LYNN
BROKEN DEEDS MC

By Esther E. Schmidt

Copyright © 2022 by Esther E. Schmidt All rights reserved.

No part of this book may be reproduced in any form,
without permission in writing from the author.

This book is a work of fiction. Incidents, names, places,
characters and other stuff mentioned in this book is the
results of the author's imagination.
Lynn Broken Deeds MC is a work of fiction.
If there is any resemblance, it is entirely coincidental.

This content is for mature audiences only. Please do not read
if sexual situations, violence and explicit language offends you.

Cover design by:
Esther E. Schmidt

Editor #1:
Christi Durbin

Editor #2:
Virginia Tesi Carey

Cover model:
Michelle Lynn McLeod

Photographer:
JW Photography and Covers
Jean Maureen Woodfin

Dedication

To all my Broken Deeds MC Readers who love Lynn;
This one's for you!

xo Esther

- 2022 -

CHAPTER ONE

LYNN

I hit the brakes and kill the engine as I park my SUV in front of the Areion Fury MC clubhouse. This was once my home about three decades ago. My brother, Zack, is still the president of this MC. Now–standing here after all those years–so much has changed.

For one I don't belong to this MC. A little over thirty years ago Deeds, the president of Broken Deeds MC at the time, claimed me. To say my brother was not happy about it was the understatement of the year. Hell, even I fought the man's claim tooth and nail, but you can't fight the inevitable and it's why I eventually fully accepted.

It would have been stupid not to when the man is my match in every way. It helps the man has the looks, the strength, the brains, the dream job, and is born to walk beside a woman like me. Though, our lives and relationship have never been smooth sailing.

Standing here now, after all this time, we still have moments in time both MCs go head-to-head. For instance, when my oldest son, Archer–who is now the president of Broken Deeds–claimed Beatrice, the daughter of Dams, the vice president of Areion Fury.

Not just the way Deeds claimed me either, my son simply knocked her up to reinforce the claim he already had in place the moment he was old enough to acknowledge his feelings. Yeah, our kids growing up and having parties, barbeques, and all…teenagers mingle, grow into adults, and get hitched.

Like I said, kids popping out and mingling because Austin is Pokey's son; Areion Fury. But Austin knocked Jersey, Ramrod's daughter, up. Ramrod is

Broken Deeds. Austin is one hell of an investigator and worked with us on active cases. Broken Deeds MC secretly works for the government to solve crime cases by using any means possible.

Yeah, our two MCs might be linked through thick and thin but recently we had an issue where my niece thought it was okay to hide a biker from Broken Deeds. One that was presumed dead. Not a smart thing to do and there was a string of false accusations and misunderstandings, causing a wedge.

The connection between MCs can be best described as the feeling between your legs after a rough night of fucking. Sore. You feel it with each step you take. Shit. I release a deep sigh. The things my mind comes up with. I blame it on the weeks of no sex.

It's all me. Deeds is still the loving, annoying, strong, perfect, asshole who claimed me many decades ago but my body has been changing, and not for the best. My period is wreaking havoc on my body and all the signs and tells of getting older suck long, wrinkly, hairy balls.

I grit my teeth at the reminder of feeling old and

swing the door open. I get out of the SUV and manage to knock my elbow against the door that's falling shut. I release a string of curses, and frustration tangles with pain, aggravation, disappointment, and anger. This is not my damn morning.

First, I overslept and had to rush out of bed. Need I mention it takes effort to get out of bed these days and that it takes more than one cup of coffee to fuel this old sack of meat and bones? I'm here to pick up my granddaughter, Queenie.

Bee asked me a few days ago if I could swing by the Areion Fury MC clubhouse Saturday morning at nine AM. Dams and Nerd let Queenie spend the night so Archer and Bee could have a date night. I'm not always the one to pick Queenie up, if Archer or Bee are in the neighborhood they will, and shoot me a message so I don't have to drag my ass out of bed.

The grandparents also switch weeks. It was my and Deeds' turn last week. We all enjoy spending time with our grandkids. Each and every one of them. I have loads. Having four kids myself gives me a lot of cheeks to squeeze. Though, I don't see all of them as much as I'd like to.

My youngest daughter, for instance, married a prince years ago and is now a fucking queen. Uh huh. Royalty. That kinda makes me queen bitch. I chuckle at my own train of thought.

"What the hell are you doing here, bitch?" a voice quips and I turn to face Blue, my best friend since forever.

Our parents lived next door to each other so we grew up together. We only had a fall out when she left the country decades ago. She and my brother had this whole teenage love thing and shit happened and they were torn apart. Cue the falling out and then they had their second chance and here we are, still best friends even if our clubs are standing in the middle of our friendship.

"That's Queen Bitch to you," I snap.

Her laughter flows through the air until it's cut off when she says, "What are you doing here this early on a Sunday morning?"

"Sunday?" I murmur. "It's Saturday and I'm supposed to pick up Queenie. She stayed with Nerd and

Dams last night."

Blue frowns. "Uhm, hate to say it…but…you're an hour early and a day late."

I roll my eyes. As if. Reaching for my phone, I fish it out of my ass-pocket and tap the screen to make it light up so I can check the date. Fuck. Me.

"What the actual fuck?" I grumble and am stunned by the fact Blue is right.

It's eight AM on this bright and early Sunday morning.

"I was at the clubhouse yesterday when Archer picked up Queenie. He was here before nine AM to drop something off for Zack and took Queenie with him. Archer said he'd let you know he already picked her up."

"Guess it slipped his mind and I have no clue what happened to mine to mix up the damn day. I'm never late, dammit," I huff and release a deep sigh before I mutter, "I'm getting too damn old."

"Pssssshhhh. This has shit to do with getting old but more to do about you taking on the world along with the universe at the same time. We're all getting older. Zack has been wanting to retire for years but it's damn hard when you have twin boys who both want to take the gavel. Then there's my bad knee and the operation has done shit so I can't even do a single workout and my ass has gotten twice as big. Do you know how hard it is to drag these curves around with a bad knee?" Blue huffs and crosses her arms in front of her chest. "Yeah, chirping birds, rays of fucking sunshine, hearts and flowers, and shit? Fairytales are in print, audio, and eBook, they do this gaggingly sweet romance shit on TV in movies and series, but the real world? That's like the boob sweat no one likes to have sliding down your stomach on a hot summer day."

"Don't remind me," I grumble. "Both the not being able to work out together the way we used to, and the damn boob sweat. It's as if I'm sweating like a pig all the damn time."

Blue leans forward and whisper hisses, "Menopause. Fucking hot flashes, mood blown to shit, and a vag that's dryer than the damn Sahara."

"Okay, we're going to end this complain-train

before it makes any more stops. My stomach can't handle it. You know, with the cortisone shots fixing the inflammation in my shoulder and with it causing new issues? See? Fucking hell, how come there's never any positive shit, huh? Dashing out of bed, cheerful as fuck, happy to face a new day without a sliver of bodily pain."

"Or have a day where you can throw your legs into the air, fold yourself into a human pretzel, loads of stamina…orgasm-train instead of the damn complain-train. Ugh, I miss the good ol'days," Blue groans.

"Me too," I mutter.

"Tequila?" she prompts.

I shrug and shove down the thought of my stomach throwing up a fit if I throw an exhilarator on the fire that's always burning inside there. "It's booze time somewhere on this planet and we're old enough not to need a damn excuse."

Turning, I open the car door and grab my purse before locking up the SUV and wander to Blue who is making her way into the clubhouse. The main room is empty, not so surprising on a Sunday morning bright and fucking early. That makes me wonder as I plant my ass on the couch and watch Blue grab a bottle of tequila from the bar along with two shot glasses.

"What are you doing up early?" I place my purse next to my feet, it's mega-size because I always need loads of stuff and also like to shove stuff in there for whenever I need it.

Blue sighs and plunks down next to me. "Club business."

I snatch the bottle from her fingers and fill the shot glasses.

Handing her one I grumble, "To us women who battle life at the cost of our own blood, flesh, bones, and mental insanity-shit."

"To mental insanity-shit," Blue echoes.

Our glasses clink in the air and we throw them back. Fuck. The burn in my throat is nice but the flaming pain in my stomach sucks balls. Blue fills our glasses again and we repeat the action a few more times.

After an hour we're leaning against one another and both of us are still rambling about shit that bothers us but at least we're laughing. The booze has done its job in easing the frustration and even my stomach pains have faded, or at least have slipped to the background.

"I think the twins are planning to kill Zack and take over as prez," Blue blurts and throws her tequila down her throat.

The booze filling my mouth almost slides down my windpipe but I manage to save myself and quickly swallow.

"Come again," I croak and smack my chest a few times as I clear my throat.

Blue slaps my back. "Okay, maybe not kill but they were not happy when he told them they can't both become president. A club doesn't have two Prezs but one and a VP. They've been going head-to-head about this shit for the past few weeks and it's insane."

"Dude, that's crazy." I frown and snatch the bottle to fill our glasses.

Blue stares into the shot glass as if she sees the answers of life bubbling to the surface. "Yeah. And I might have been so sick of the whole bumping heads thing, I might have told Zack to step down and let those fuckers run the MC the way they want to because it's their time so he needs to let go."

We both wince at the same time and I mutter, "I can only imagine how well that went."

"At least being up for hours earned me to catch your pretty face bright and early." She holds up her glass and we clink them together before throwing it back.

"Handing over the gavel is a monumental thing. Archer and Deeds faced issues beyond club business, and it was simply time without a choice. Zack, on the other hand, has no reason to step down. He's still fierce as fuck and he's the one who molded how the club is running now. If he hands it over, it is literally out of his hands. His twins will still hold the same mindset." I give her a soft smile. "I know all of you. They are my family too, even though I belong to another club I'd still bleed Areion Fury as well when my blood is spilled. Though we all know we have to let everyone live their own life and it's only possible by letting them take their own path. If they stumble? Let them fucking faceplant to make them feel the burn of the scrapes or get their teeth knocked out. So, you're both right. You for letting your old man know when it's time to let go but Zack for wanting to protect the club. But my vote is to let those twins crash teeth-first into the asphalt."

"Fucking hell, sis," Zack grumbles.

I whirl around to face my brother and the room spins a little faster due to this action and the booze combined.

"How long have you been standing there?" I snap. "Ears flapping and all? Doesn't make you any prettier because men always get longer ears the older they get and yours almost touch your shoulders."

He completely ignores my sneer about his ears.

"Long enough to hear my old lady spill club business." He stalks to Blue and I'm on my feet to block his path with my next breath.

Jabbing my finger against his chest I bite out the

words, "She didn't spill club business, asshole. She threw a much needed load off her shoulders. One that blocks both of you and that shit burns in the pit of your stomach. Acid. Something you don't need when you're not getting any younger and I can tell by the fatigue below your eyes it's dragging you down as well. Deeds might not be prez anymore and Bee took over as the president's old lady when my son took over but that doesn't mean my job or Deeds' was done the second that gavel passed hands. Fuck, no. You pass on a legacy and let them shape it the way you did when you took over from our father. It's inevitable and needed because time doesn't stop. There was once a time folks thought the earth was flat but it's round as fuck. See? Just roll with it old man and let your sons take on the world and explore whatever the future holds for them." I step back and mutter, "It frees up your schedule to spend some more time with your old lady. Maybe even fuck her against the wall or throw her legs into the air and fold her like a pretzel. Forget your own mindset when it's locked on the past while your blood wants to broaden their horizons and build their own future."

I grab the bottle of tequila and bring it to my mouth to swallow down the last few sips. I have to sidestep to keep my balance. Shit. I've passed the point of tipsy. Time to go home. Turning, I notice Zack is holding Blue in his arms and is kissing the shit out of her. Great. At least she's getting some action.

A biker strolls into the room and I know who the young fucker is. He's the spitting image of his father. Before Sico claimed his old lady he was a complete manwhore. The phrase "Like father, like son," slips through my mind. At least the idiot has the looks to maintain a nice stream of girls sparking interest in the fucker.

"You," I grunt and point the empty bottle at Briggs. "You're taking me home."

A sly, sexy smile slides across his face. "I'm down for some cougar action if you are."

I flip the bottle of tequila in my hand and instantly have it ready to knock him over the head with it. I swing my arm back but the weight of the bottle suddenly disappears.

"None of that, sis. Time to go home," Zack says. "Briggs, rein it in and get Deeds' old lady home. I don't have to give you another damn warning to keep it in your pants because my sister will kick your ass if you don't behave. Fuck. Maybe Deeds will put you six feet under if he gets wind of you being down for some…fuck, I can't even repeat that shit."

Blue shoots me a grin and I find myself chuckling. Yeah, my morning might have started shitty but I'm feeling fucking fine now.

CHAPTER TWO

DEEDS

I'm standing in front of the clubhouse when I see my old lady's SUV coming around the corner. She's not behind the wheel, Briggs is. The little punk. Sico and Everleigh's son was just patched in. According to Zack, he's a pain in the ass but a loyal one.

The SUV comes to a stop and a truck pulls in behind it. Ryno, Tyler and Ridley's son, jumps out and gives me a chin lift. He crosses his arms over his chest and leans back against the truck to wait for Briggs so they can both head back to the Areion Fury clubhouse.

I wander to the SUV and open the door of the

passenger side. Lips gives me a beaming smile and throws her purse over her shoulder before sliding out. She's about to say something but her eyes go over my shoulder. Her lips pucker while her eyes narrow and I can see the fire inside them flaming into an inferno.

She shoves her purse against my abs and snarls, "Hold this."

Before I can say or do anything she dashes around me and fucking buries her fist against Briggs' eye.

His head whips back and the man chuckles. "Oh, come on now, babe. I'm all about a little foreplay and mixing pain with pleasure. So, you'd better give me a little sugar now too."

What. The. Fuck?

Lips spins around, grabs her purse from my hands and shoves her arm–elbow deep–inside, and pulls out a damn hammer. Who the hell carries a damn hammer in their purse? You think you know a woman when you've been together for decades, but my old lady never ceases to amaze me.

"Get the fuck in the truck, brother," Ryno

bellows. "Now."

Briggs laughs and jumps in as Ryno peels out. I can barely wrap my arm around Lips to prevent her from chasing the truck. I can't stop her from throwing the hammer, though. It whirls through the air and hits the back window of the truck before it lands in the truck bed.

"What the hell is going on?" I growl and let go of my woman.

She whirls around and grits through her teeth, "That idiot hits me." She frowns. "On me." A huff of frustration rips from her. "Fucking hits on me."

My woman is one of a kind. I chuckle at the mere sight and the fierce way she always handles her shit. The moment I do is when I know I've fucked up. The glare I get tells me as much. Lips snatches her purse off the ground and stomps toward the clubhouse.

Bumping against my shoulder she snaps, "Thanks for the kick in the vag, asshole. It's rarely seen action as it is, and I really needed to know my old man thinks the skin on my bones is too wrinkly to catch someone's attention."

"Now wait just a goddamned minute," I grumble but she's shoving her hand into the air and gives me the finger. "You mistook my expression for something else, dammit."

It doesn't matter what I say because she's already slamming the door behind her. My frustration is running on overload when I grab my phone out of my pocket. I thumb the screen and find Zack's number.

He picks up on the third ring. "Did my sister get home okay?"

"I want Briggs' balls in a damn jar." I stomp into the clubhouse.

Zack's deep sigh flows into my ear. "What did that asshole do now?"

"Hit on your damn sister and caused a misunderstanding so my old lady now thinks I don't believe her when she told me he hit on her. She fucking thinks that I fucking think she isn't hot enough." Stepping inside the clubhouse I whip my head around but find the room empty. Heading into the hallway so I can go out back I tell Zack, "I'm not shitting you, Zack. The fist to the eye Lynn gave him isn't enough.

And you can damn well keep the hammer she threw through the back window of Ryno's truck. The fucker is damn lucky she missed his head."

Zack releases a string of curses. "I'm so damn tired of this shit. My sister is right. Hell, my old lady is right. I'm stepping down and letting my twins handle these idiots. I've reprimanded that asshole so many times he's indefinitely carrying an imprint of my boot on his ass, but nothing makes a damn difference. Just like my twins, hard-headed and they all think they know better."

"Hate saying 'I told you so' but we both know the second generation we helped put on this world are green behind the ears and it's time they find out just how fucked-up life can get. So, make sure those twins put Briggs' balls in a jar and send them to me." I don't wait for a reply, but I hang up and shove my phone back into my pocket when I burst through the front door of my house.

I scan the living room and come up empty. There's a slight noise coming from the kitchen and my feet automatically move in that direction.

Coming to a stop in the doorway to see her sitting on one of the kitchen chairs, her hand is on the table, covered with a bag of frozen peas.

The defeat in her gaze when her eyes find mine? Fucking gut-wrenching. There's no way she'll let me fuss over her nor will she accept any words I give her right now. It's for this reason I make my hands busy with making some coffee. As soon as I have a cup in hand, I place it in front of her on the table.

She glares at me. "Give the bitch some caffeine to sober up, huh?"

Lifting the bag of peas, I glance at her hand. Fuck. Her knuckles are all red and swollen and it's the damn hand she was shot in a few months ago. I've been shot in the hand twice and had a knife go through it as well. I needed surgery months after everything to regain function; I know how fucked-up the healing process is.

"You should have let me punch the fucker," I growl and bring her knuckles closer to my face to brush a kiss against the angry red skin. Pulling back, I ramble, "Fuck it. I'm going over there right now to kick his damn ass. Zack might have decided to pass the gavel over to his twins to let the second generation handle those young stallions, but the fucker needs to face the consequences of trying, or so much as thinking, he can get a taste of what's mine."

She inches her knuckles closer to my lips and raises her well-groomed eyebrow. The corner of my mouth threatens to twitch but I manage to cover it up by placing a kiss on my woman's hand.

"Did my brother tell you he's stepping down?" she questions.

I place another kiss on her knuckles. "He said as much when I called him to demand he'd send me that fucker's balls in a jar."

Finally, the grin I like to see on her face slides in place. "Nice."

She takes her hand back and wraps both around the mug and takes a sip from the coffee I made her. I can tell she's not fully using her injured hand and I hate seeing any signs of discomfort on her, but I know it's there.

I also know for damn sure not to bring it up. Hell,

I've been trying to get her to slow her roll for years now, but she keeps going without so much as taking a day off. The reality of having her burn straight through her energy is a vivid fear of mine.

My woman is a badass but that doesn't mean she'd be less of one if she'd throw some responsibilities on others. Fucking hell, I thought me stepping down as president would also mean my old lady would have less on her plate.

Instead, she keeps her head high above anyone else's and has the widest shoulders to carry any type of burden no matter whose it is. Her spine is made out of steel but the wear and tear over the years can easily break the unbreakable. I guess that's my fear; losing her before I expel my last breath.

I clear my throat and decide to switch topics and shove my thoughts and the confrontation away and tell her, "I stole a case off our son's desk. When I glanced through the file, I thought it might interest you."

A low chuckle slips over her pouty lips. "Devious, stealing a case. Well, you sure have my interest spiked so give me all the deets, Deeds."

I shake my head and release my own chuckle as I stroll into the living room to retrieve the file. When I return Lips drains the last of her coffee and rinses her cup in the sink before returning to her seat at the kitchen table.

She holds out her hand, rapidly opening and closing it. "Gimme."

Handing it over I start to explain, "It's not so much a string of dead bodies, blood, gore, and mayhem. More leaning toward an angel of mercy, angel of death, kind of thing. Actually, as you can see in the note you're holding, Ivy is the one who connected the deaths."

Ivy is Chopper's old lady, she's an ER doctor and a nurse from the hospital approached her with some concerns about sudden deaths. Even if some of the kids were undergoing chemo, deaths were sudden and unexplainable, as are a handful of older folks dying all of a sudden while they were ready to be discharged. Lips spreads the photographs and documents out in front of her and I make a quick trip to the living room to grab her reading glasses.

As soon as I'm strolling back into the kitchen she murmurs, "Mind getting my–"

She doesn't have to finish her sentence because I'm already holding the glasses out for her to take. Lips takes them without looking up and slides them on. Fuck. My woman knocks the breath from my lungs no matter the time of day or what she's wearing.

Beauty can hold different levels for everyone, but Lips increases the mere definition and develops a unique brand of it just by being the complete person she is. Yeah, every inch and cell of my body and mind is still consumed by this woman. Even after roughly three decades, through fights, kids, grandkids, enemies, club shit, injuries, or whatever life has thrown at us in spades; our bond is unbreakable.

Her long, dirty blonde hair turned to a more silver color over time and it suits her perfectly. The red ink of the Broken Deeds MC patch on her neck still makes my damn heart skip each time I catch a glimpse of it. I love her so damn much.

Lips checks her watch. "Ivy already left for her shift at the hospital?"

She scoops all the papers back up and places them into the file.

"I've asked Ivy to swing by tomorrow morning. With this being Sunday and her working, I thought it was easier. That reminds me, why were you up this early and over at the Areion Fury clubhouse?"

Lips clenches and unclenches her fist, and I can tell by the wince on her face it's still bugging her.

Releasing a deep sigh she mutters, "I thought I had to pick up Queenie but once I was there Blue told me I was an hour early and a day late. Archer should have mentioned it to me yesterday that he picked her up himself. But how the fuck did I mix up the day or the time for that matter?"

Within a few strides, I'm standing behind her and gently slide her long hair from her back to massage her shoulders. "Archer should have mentioned something yesterday. Then it wouldn't have happened. Though, from what I heard, you and Blue both needed some girl time. Even if there was tequila before ten AM involved."

"Not just Blue. Zack needed some verbal lashing to knock some sense into him." She groans and lets her head fall forward. "Keep going. Feels good."

Damn right it feels good. It's been way too long since I had my hands on her. With everything going on with the club, family, us, life…time simply slips away. Also the reason why I told her Archer should have said something and that she and Blue needed to spend some time together. I want to tell her she should take a step back and let others handle their own shit.

Like hell will I ever mention that to her; she'd rip my cock straight off and throw it in my face while chewing on my balls like she's popping gum. I don't fear my woman–everyone else might–I just like my cock and balls to remain where they are.

Besides, my woman will always be fierce, loyal, dedicated, and ready to take on the world while she's already carrying the universe on her fucking shoulders. But it would be good to take it a bit slow.

Quite the contradiction for me to throw a case

at her to give her more things to do but the truth is, when she's working on a case, she's focused on solving it rather than worrying about all the kids, grandkids, old ladies, club brothers, and everything else.

I'm hoping my plan works. Otherwise, I'll put my cock and balls at risk. Either by fucking her into oblivion or handing them over as I tell her straight up she needs to calm her tits to slow her roll; the way her body is also telling her to.

We're not getting any younger and the way she's running through life leaves little energy to save for the many years we still have on this fucked-up planet.

CHAPTER THREE

LYNN

I blink a few times and slowly become alive to the world once again. Keyword being slowly with all the aches my old bones are screaming inside my brain about. I mutter a few curses to force myself into action as I get to my feet.

I hear people talking and I'm guessing someone is talking to Deeds inside our house. I'll worry about that later; pee first, face the issues of the world after. I handle my business while kickstarting my brain as I wonder what day today is.

Right. Monday. Lynette, my youngest daughter, and her husband, Windsor, are taking their son,

Xavier to school. First day for those young parents and kid. I hate not being there but it's their moment. My grandson is going to be a king one day.

Hell, I still can't believe Lynette fell in love with a prince. All while the man didn't know he had royal blood running inside his veins. Of course, it was tainted with mafia blood but Windsor never dipped a toe in that side of the family. Spence, my youngest son, has his own Broken Deeds MC chapter in New Jersey.

Lynette used to be a part of it and they handle undercover cases while our chapter, well, the one my oldest son is now president of, handles cold cases or urgent cases the government needs solved as soon as possible. Windsor was an undercover case. Lynette literally ran into Windsor before she even knew he was a damn case.

Call it fate or whatever but those two belong together. Sucks that they live on an island called Ryckerdan where Windsor is now king and my daughter the fucking queen. It's a gorgeous island. I fucking hate getting sand in my butt but fucking love to watch the waves crash against the sandy beach.

Yeah, I'm proud as fuck of that young family and love visiting them but it's bittersweet not to be able to have them close all the time the way Archer and Bee are living right here. He and his old lady are running the chapter in their own way…just like Deeds and I once did.

Then there's my oldest daughter, Esmee. She moved across the country with that CIA asshole who tried to infiltrate our MC by using her. In the end, there was nothing to investigate and those two are perfect for one another but again…across the country. No grandchildren from those two within hugging distance.

Spence is a few hours away by car so I also manage, but I guess there's nothing to complain about when I can still video call them. They're all happy, expanding their families and living their lives; exactly the way they should.

Pictures and videos. I'll get them for sure later today from Lynette. I can feel the corners of my lips tip up at the thought of seeing Xavier striding into class with his leather jacket and biker boots I bought him. That little dude might be royalty, but he loves riding the mini dirt bike Deeds and I bought him and taught him to ride. Gotta teach them the good shit as soon as they can walk.

I'm ready to face the day when I'm dressed in blue jeans, a black leather belt, a black tight shirt, and black boots. Closing the lock of my thick silver chain necklace, I grab my phone and keys to put them safely into my pocket. I fluff my hair into place and stroll out of the bedroom to head for the living room.

Obviously, my asshole husband doesn't notice me when he tells Archer, "Can't you ask Bee to oversee that shit? She's the president's old lady. Your mother should take a step back while Bee takes one forward. We're not as young as we used to be and I–"

"And you what? Can't get it up anymore because your ego is weighing down on it?" I snarl.

Both Deeds and Archer's head whip my way. I grab my black leather jacket off the coatrack and scoop up my purse as I glare at my husband and son.

"Newsflash, I might be old but I ain't dead yet," I snap and walk out the door, letting it slam shut with force behind me.

Taking the keys from my pocket, I press the car fob and open the door to throw my purse on the passenger side and hop into my SUV. I start the damn thing and hit the gas right before Deeds rushes out of the house. Just in time for him to admire my middle finger I'm waving in the air.

Asshole. How dare he? Take a fucking step back? Not as young as we used to be? Asshole! As if I need the reminder. I have no clue what they were discussing or why they were talking but come the fuck on. He has no right to decide shit for me.

Once I'm a few blocks away I park along the side of the road and reach for my phone to shoot a quick message to Ivy, telling her I'll be at the diner across town and give her the address. I want to talk through some of the things I read in the case Deeds gave me last night.

Asshole. Fury still burns hot inside my veins. Deep down I know he probably thinks he has reasons to say that shit to our son–his president. But I'll set him straight as soon as I've conquered the need to squeeze and spin his balls around to hear his voice go up a few notches.

Maybe Deeds thinks I need to take things slow because of what happened yesterday. I never should have mentioned the whole 'hour early and a day late' incident. The fucker might think I'm losing my mind or am in the middle of a burnout or some shit.

Add the fact my hand still hurts like a bitch and doesn't function right…well, it worked fine when I was using it to punch but damn was that a big mistake. Now I have pain shooting up my arm when I so much as move it as I turn the wheel.

Dammit. I need to research the internet to see if there are some vitamins or supplements to boost my joints, muscles, or whatever. Wait. I'll ask Ivy, she'll know being an ER doc and all. I finally make the turn to the parking lot of the diner and pick a spot to park my SUV. The scent of fresh coffee and pastries hits my nose as soon as I step inside.

"Hey, Lynn. The usual?" the voice of an angel

asks me.

I let my eyes find Alouette, the redhead who owns the place. She's twenty-two and just inherited this place from her mother.

"Yeah, chickie. How are you this morning?" I question.

She sighs overdramatically. "Do you see this face? I have to maintain this smile so people think I give a fuck while I make sure to fill their orders while all I want is a man with big hands and a big dick to take good care of me. But even that is too much to ask these days."

I shoot the chick a grin. This is why I keep coming for coffee. She doesn't have a filter and speaks her mind no matter what. Clients are used to it and if not, they put up with it because she's a badass barista and one hell of a cook. Her muffins, cake, pie, anything she bakes is damn good.

"Why the big hands, Lou?" I find myself asking.

One of her eyebrows hits the ceiling. "To rub my feet after working the whole damn day of course. My pussy ain't the only one wanting relief after a hard day's work."

"Ain't that the truth," I agree and stalk off to my favorite spot in the back of the diner and place my back to the wall so I can oversee everything.

Dropping my bag at my feet, I take out my phone and ignore the flashy notifications of my asshole man and son. I only click on the text Ivy sent me and smile to know she'll be here in twenty minutes. Perfect. It'll give me time to enjoy a caramel cinnamon muffin and my damn coffee.

"Here you go, sweets," Lou tells me and glances over her shoulder to check if the girl she hired to help her out is handling things.

I get the feeling she's lingering to ask me something, so I blurt, "Well, sit your ass down if you want to talk. I know you have a mouth on you and ain't afraid to use it so out with it already."

"Fine," she huffs and plunks down in the booth across from me. "Remember, you asked, okay?"

I shrug and take my coffee in hand as I lean back. "Lay it on me, Lou."

"You've shared some things when you're here

working and…well, I would like to hire you."

Blinking a few times, I have to kickstart my brain and wonder why she would want to hire me. I come here a lot to enjoy a moment to myself and rarely share this location with anyone else. Hell, Deeds doesn't know I swing by here and it's for good reason too; I need my own space to take a minute when needed.

He has his brothers; I have this diner and Lou to take a moment to myself. Yes, I have the other old ladies to fall back on and I also search them out when I need them, but this place is for me and my sanity. I have no other explanation.

Lou is also right about me sharing some things. I sometimes have files with me to go over a case I'm working on. Most times I take low-profile cases, missing persons, cold cases that need dusting off and write notes so a brother can take over and check out leads, that type of stuff.

When Lou asked me what I did for a living I told her I moonlighted as a private investigator from time to time. It's an easy and safe explanation that doesn't give away too much about me or the club.

"Why do you want to hire me?" I prod.

"To find my biological father." She bites her bottom lip and glances at her new waitress again before finding my gaze. "I don't have much to go on. Just a first name, where he used to work, and where he lived when my mother was seeing him."

Ugh, this girl. She's never asked me for anything, always has an ear free for me to throw out my frustrations of life and is as sweet as they come while standing strong during whirlwinds. Because running this diner isn't peanuts and she does it flawlessly.

Decision made.

Over her shoulder I notice Ivy strolling into the diner and I quickly tell Lou, "Write everything you know down and give it to me. I'll let you know what I find."

Lou gives me a relieved smile. "Thank you," she tells me and rises to her feet to come to a stop right next to me.

"Thank me with a muffin and coffee when I find something," I reply and add with a stern voice,

"That's all the payment I request, got me?"

"For a whole month," she shoots back and immediately holds up her hand. "I insist. No one works for free. Besides, I like having you come around more than you already do. With losing my mother, I don't have any family and only work my ass off here. I like to think we're friends, even if you're a paying customer."

Ivy slides into the booth Lou was sitting in and watches me while I tell Lou, "I'm here for you, chickie. Not only for the damn fine coffee and baked goods." Now it's me who is holding up my hand. "Yeah, I don't do hugs so let's not do that unless someone dies or one of us is dying a bit on the inside, okay?"

Her sweet laughter flows through the air and mixes with Ivy's.

Lou's attention slides to Ivy. "Hi, I'm Lou, what can I get you?"

"Ivy. I'll have an espresso and a bagel, please."

Ivy gets a genuine smile after Lou lets her know, "Coming right up."

As soon as Lou is out of earshot Ivy tells me, "Why do I get the feeling you meeting me here isn't random and you've been keeping this place all to yourself?"

I snort. "Because I don't like sharing my secret hideaway. Kinda blows the whole sneaking away for a serene coffee moment to shit. So, don't say anything to anyone."

I have to bite my lip to ask her if she was followed but I decide to leave it. Deeds probably will wait for me to blow off my aggravation and expects me to come home later anyway. Which I always do. Duh. Shit gets hard no matter where in life we are, but that man has been my rock through tornadoes, landslides, shootouts, killings, and what the fuck else–was and is–thrown our way.

"My lips are sealed," Ivy states and at the same time Lou strides to the table to quickly place Ivy's order in front of her before slinking away.

I let Ivy talk me through her reasons of reporting some deaths in the hospital after a nurse came to her with her findings. I shoot a couple of questions in return and after half an hour I'm itching to start going through the files I left at home.

Ivy needs to be back at the hospital later and we say our goodbyes after she placed another order to take with her. Yeah, I have a feeling Ivy will drive across town to get her coffee and bagel from now on. Lou is simply that good with her baking and coffee.

Lou hands me another coffee to go and I swing my purse over my shoulder as I take the note from her. I scan the things she wrote about her biological father and it's not much to go on but worth a try nonetheless.

I'm giving her a finger wave as I stroll to the door, a smile on my face as I go. Yeah, my mood is way better than it was when I got here. Though, when the sunlight hits my face, my mood quickly sours when I spot Deeds leaning against my SUV.

CHAPTER FOUR

DEEDS

I keep leaning against her SUV–my legs crossed at the ankles, and my thumbs casually hooked into the loops of my jeans–as I watch my woman stride out of the building. Her long gray hair flows through the wind as she waves to the woman in the diner.

Her jeans are hugging her curves, the leather jacket she always wears suits her perfectly, but it's the careless smile tugging her fuckable lips that makes my cock hard. I know this place is where she comes to have a coffee break.

She might think it's her best kept secret but I'm the one who cleans her car every few weeks and there have been loads of empty coffee cups and empty bags in there with this diner's name on them. I hate the way her smile slides right off when she spots me.

"What are you doing here? Nothing better to do than to track down my ass by following Ivy?" she grumbles.

Instead of throwing words at her, I push away from the SUV and stalk right up to her. Sliding my hand around her throat to cup the back of her neck, I angle her head the way I need it and slam my mouth over hers. It's one of the few and rare ways I know how to shut my woman up.

My tongue demands entrance and she opens for me while at the same time her body melts against mine. Fucking perfect. The past few weeks have been hectic as fuck and we've barely had time to be together other than our heads hitting the pillow for a few hours a night.

The feel of her tongue piercing rubbing against me is exhilarating. She's removed the snakebite piercings–a metal stud on each side of her bottom lip near the corners of her mouth–she's had them for decades. The only time she's taken them out is when there are babies around. First our own kids and now our grandkids.

Babies have grabby hands and she's always been the kind of person who shoves her head into their bellies to blow raspberries. She just doesn't want the fuss and would shave her hair as well, but I guess she draws the line…or I do because I love her long hair, even if it changed from dirty blonde to silver gray.

I brush her silk hair away and trail a path of kisses to the side of her neck where my name is inked in the patch. Fuck, decades of seeing it on my favorite part of her skin to nip and suck and it never gets old to see it.

Her breath is hot right next to my ear and the feel of her fists buried in my leather cut is spiking the need to spin her around and fuck her against the SUV. Man, it's been way too long since I've buried myself in her sweet little pussy.

My hands sneak down to her ass and I knead it

while grinding my pelvis against hers, making her feel what she does to me. I swallow down the moan and slowly turn her to press her against the SUV, caging her in.

With Lips it always feels as if I'm playing with fire. The heat from her body, hot lashes from her mouth, and the inferno my cock is surrounded with when I bury myself deep inside her. Mag-fucking-nificent.

It takes effort to make my brain function through the lust-haze it's clogged with, but I manage to open the side door and hoist my woman inside. Thank fuck for the overload on space in this interior but it's still a pain to strip off her tight jeans and place her underneath me as I fumble with my own damn zipper.

"Get inside me already," Lips demands and licks those well-kissed lips of hers.

I fist my cock and slide it against her pussy. Instead of entering her in one stroke, I use short and determined strokes to get inside her heat. Both our bodies have changed. Fucking raw and hard takes a little preparation.

Dripping wet isn't what her body gives me but she's slick enough to let me tease her pussy to give me an in and show it's still mine to fuck and pleasure. In return my cock isn't the steel pipe that can go for multiple rounds, nor does my body have the same stamina to keep going for a long period of time.

Doesn't mean it's bad. Doesn't mean we can't do it; we simply adjust and still make it fucking work. And daaaaamn, being fully lodged inside her has the both of us groaning loud. I bury my head into the crook of her neck and scrape my teeth over her skin.

It's my favorite spot on her body and I know for a fact it affects her just as much as me. The reminder comes in the clenching of her pussy around my cock. Fucking hell, I've missed this. My hips start to pump and Lips is moving underneath me, shoving her tight heat on and off my cock as if it's a damn contest of who gets who off first.

I'm balancing myself on one hand and sneak my other one between our bodies until I find her bundle of nerves. All it takes is a little rubbing and pressure and she lights up like a Christmas tree; bursting colorful lights through the air to light up the whole damn house. Well, in this case the inside of the SUV as she pulls me right over the edge.

Cum rips from my body and I'm riding an orgasm bliss just as hard as her. I'm biting her shoulder, sucking her skin to leave my mark while I hear my name being moaned right beside my ear.

This. Right here. Me and my woman and nothing else. It's been a long fucking time since we had this together but it's also much needed. When you live together for years, raise a family, run a business, have a solid brotherhood, it simply leaves little time to divide for the crucial elements that are the foundation in your whole damn life.

"Mind covering your ass and stepping out of the vehicle?" a voice rumbles from behind me, breaking this special moment I have with my woman.

A dose of "pissed-the-fuck-off" hits me full force and by the sound of "what the fuck?" coming from my woman's lips I'd say it hit us both at the same time.

I brush my mouth against my old lady's lips and murmur, "Ready to fuck this asshole up for interrupting?"

"You know I'm always ready to go batshit crazy, love," she fucking croons.

"Love you so damn much, woman," I fiercely tell her and crash my mouth against hers.

The clearing of a throat annoys me but doesn't make me stop, even if the man grits, "Now would be a good time."

I slowly pull out of the slice of heaven between my woman's legs and make sure to block the view of whomever is standing behind me. When I'm sure Lips has pulled on her jeans and is buttoning up, I slowly turn to the fucker who interrupted the best sex we've had in months.

"Hands behind your back, sir," the cop that looks still green behind his ears informs me. "Lewd conduct in public, the law prohibits it. You and the prostitute are being arrested. You have the right–"

Prostitute? Motherfucker. He doesn't get the chance to ramble off my rights nor has a chance to throw cuffs on me because I'm beating the shit out of him the next damn second. I'm straddling the fucker when I'm being hit with a jolt of electricity and my whole body seizes.

My body stops working and I turn to see Lips punch the other cop who tasered me. She's about to swing again but with my next breath the both of us are being held at gunpoint by the cop I was straddling.

A few minutes later Lips and I are sitting handcuffed in the back of a squad car, grinning like teenagers who just pulled a prank. My smile doesn't fade one goddamned bit for the hours that pass and sure as fuck brightens some more when I finally walk out of the precinct and see Archer leaning against his bike.

"Where's your mom?" I question.

My son's mouth is set in a straight line and my brother, Broke, is standing right next to him and tells me, "Lips is waiting for you at home. She was released an hour before you were. Archer here had to swing by himself to get you out and make them drop the charges because you assaulted a cop. Broke his damn nose."

I shrug. "Should teach him not to fuck with me and my woman."

I keep the part where the cop called his mother a prostitute to myself. If I did tell him? He'd march right into that precinct himself to give the cop two black eyes along with his broken nose.

"Or you could stick to keeping your shit in the bedroom. You're grandparents for fuck's sake," Archer grumbles. "A son shouldn't bail out their parents for sexual conduct in a public place."

Yeah, for sure as fuck my smile is still in place when I tell him, "Why not? It shows how much your mother still means to me."

Archer shakes his head and straddles his bike. "Maybe your nephew can bail you out next time because I'm not doing it again."

He rides off and Broke chuckles. "My kid would have done it if he wasn't out on a case. You should have seen the look on Archer's face when he got the call from Kessie."

I chuckle. Kessie Ansel is our government contact.

She reaches out whenever something comes across her desk that either links with our cases or any member of Broken Deeds MC. Kessie always has her panties in a twist when it comes to my woman, so I bet she gave Archer an earful when she called to inform him his parents got themselves arrested.

Taking my keys from my pocket I straddle my Harley and fire it up. "I couldn't care less, brother. I've never felt so alive as I do in this moment. Like the good old days where you and I were Prez and VP instead of my son and yours being in our shoes now. Though, clearly, we were more badass. At least we wouldn't complain if we had to bust out anyone for fucking his old lady."

Broke throws his head back and barks out a laugh. "True that, bro. True that."

I guide my bike onto the road and head home. The wind hitting me, scenery flashing by, darkness surrounding me while my heart feels bright as fuck, is damn near perfection. This morning when Lips rushed out of the house when she heard me stepping up for her, along with the day before where we collided for the same reason, now feels different.

When we first started out, she fought my claim tooth and nail. Her being an MC president's daughter, being raised in an MC and her brother taking over all while she would have been president if she had a cock makes her the strong woman she is.

My damn counterpart but it also means we occasionally go head-to-head. Each of us has a strong character and our own mindset to handle shit. I hate seeing her in pain and struggling to keep up with everything going on these days while I should have never doubted her.

Going behind her back to protect her wasn't a good idea and I used to sidestep issues by making it seem like some shit was her idea to do it differently instead. Like the way I gave her a case to focus on to make sure she threw some other jobs off her schedule.

I know she likes to babysit all the kids, no matter if they are our own grandbabies or anyone else's in the club. Though, it drains her. She also keeps an eye out for all the old ladies, along with the brothers, making sure they don't work their ass off. She's the fucking glue that holds this MC together.

I park my bike and jog toward the house, itching to get to my woman. Opening the door, I get hit by the incredible scent of lasagna. My woman has been cooking. Striding into the kitchen I'm just in time to see her pull some fresh baked Italian bread from the oven.

"Sit," she orders me with a huge grin on her face. "I made you some extra calories. Figured you'd come home hungry and all."

"You always know what's good for me, love," I croon and grab her neck to gain access to her hot lips.

I take her mouth in a fierce kiss to show her how much I love the gesture, the time we spend together, fuck…even getting arrested and getting home to this. Our kiss seals the love we still have burning hot through our veins.

It might have once stayed on the back burner, but it doesn't mean it lost its spark. Fuck, no. Love is like a thick line that can either be erased, wear thinner, or gain thickness. With us it consists of layers, adding on another layer when it needs a reminder of the foundation.

Hard-headed, colliding, throwing curses back and forth; everyone has a unique combination and not one is the same when it comes to relationships. Ours is unusual but strong enough to conquer life itself no matter what obstacles we face.

CHAPTER FIVE

LYNN

I'm wearing a grin as I take out my notepad and reading glasses. My plan worked flawlessly. Deeds is snoring on the couch after I put him in a food coma. How could I not? The man grabbed me and put a spin on my day, mood, feelings and gave me clarity in my messy thoughts.

Not to mention, it felt fucking good to be getting into shit together like the old days. Bee had to pick me up from the police station because Archer felt too weird to come by himself. Then I made him pick up his father by telling him he needed to be there himself to have the charges dropped.

Of course, that wasn't needed because Kessie already took care of it as soon as she received the notification we were arrested. Though, it was fun to make Archer head over to the police station.

I take a seat at the table and slide the file in front of me that holds the documents of the case I'm working on. I've already made some calls, one to the coroner to run a check on a hunch I have. Shifting in my seat gives me the reminder I'm still sore from being well used by my man. Damn, it's been awhile.

Not only to have sex but the whole "out in the open, not caring where we are, completely consumed by one another," has been missing from our lives ever since our kids grew into adults.

I'm chuckling as I reach for a pen, but it ends when my phone starts to buzz on the table. I have it on silent but the vibrations indicate I have an incoming call. Frowning, I glance at the time and reach to answer it.

I quickly step into the hallway and snap, "Talk."

"Hey, it's Liah. Can we talk?" she asks in a defeated tone.

Liah is Kray and Vienna's youngest daughter. They also have twin boys, Luke and Louie. Though, I say boys but those two are members of Broken Deeds MC and hardly boys anymore. Vienna's twin sister is married to North. Kray and North are club brothers and are considered the first generation.

Liah wanted to make a name for herself without the Broken Deeds MC link and it's why she moved across the country to study and eventually train to become the best sniper. She succeeded at a young age and I wonder why she's reaching out to me.

"Sure, what's up, girl?" I tell her in a firm but kind voice, "You know I'm always here for you."

I can hear her throat bob through the fucking phone and I instinctively know what she's about to say is going to suck ass.

"I took a hit today. Bullet in my arm that they had to surgically remove. I don't know…I can't…they are not sure if I will regain full function."

Motherfucker. I'm glad I manage to keep the curse inside my head. I know she doesn't need to hear anger and frustration. Nor does she need pity or cuddling because she's on the phone with me and I'm guessing she's hating herself for getting hit and making the call to return home.

"That fucking stinks," I grunt. "Did they give you the good stuff? Not in any pain, are you? Tell me what you need, and I'll move heaven and earth to get it done. You know I got you, babe."

"Can you let everyone know what happened? Dammit. I don't even know what happened. One second I'm getting ready to take out a target and the next I'm the one who's taken out." She releases a deep sigh. "Anyway. I'm not able to travel for the next few days but I'm going to move back home. What other damn choice do I have?"

"Lots. You hear me, bitch?" I snap.

Bitch is my go-to endearment and I've been there since the day she was born so Liah knows exactly what I mean when I call her out on the self-pity. She doesn't need to talk herself down when life throws her a curveball.

"You come home to lick your wounds and then we'll figure out what's next for you. Don't make any decisions or let your mind slip into a dark hole. We're all here for you and for sure as fuck are we going to find out who hurt you. First things first. You need to heal; mind and body. Don't worry about your Ma and your aunt. I'm going to make sure no one gives you shit about coming home. Besides, you know no one will but that's something you struggled with when you hopped out of state." I wince at the last sentence I just threw out and have to end on a happier note so I tell her, "At least now you get to bug those twin brothers of yours. Hey, maybe you finally have time to go out on a date. Flirt with one of the club brothers."

"Lips," Liah scolds but I hear the hint of laughter in the way she says my name.

"Okay, sit tight sweet-cheeks. Like I said, make sure they give you the good stuff that knocks you out so you can sleep without any pain, okay?"

"Thanks, Lips," she murmurs.

"Always, Liah. Always. Now, I'm gonna make a few calls so be ready to answer when your Ma calls. I'll make sure everyone stays put until you're ready to come home."

"You're a lifesaver," she murmurs. "Love you, Lips."

"Love you right back, darlin'."

We end the call and I have to take a deep breath to calm myself. Dammit. So much for sitting down to work on my case. Here I thought I could squeeze in an hour later to search for Lou's father as well but I guess everything has to be put on hold.

I shove my phone into my pocket and silently tiptoe back into the room to write a little note to Deeds in case he wakes up. Grabbing my keys, I shrug on my jacket and head out. The ride to Kray and North's place takes a while.

Those two are inseparable and it's pretty damn cool they managed to fall for twin sisters who are inseparable as well. Needless to say, they own two houses that are mirrored versions of each other; they're together in their own place. I park in front of Kray's place and they must have spotted me on the camera already because the front door swings open.

"Everything alright?" Kray rumbles as soon as

my ass is out of my SUV.

"Yeah. But can you get everyone together? I'd like to run some shit by you folks," I tell him and he nods, leaving the door open for me as he takes out his phone and taps the screen.

We both wander into the living room and North, Vienna, and Reva stroll out of another hallway.

"Hey," I quip and point at the couch. "Mind taking a seat?"

Reva places her feet firmly on the floor and crosses her arms. "Just tell us why you're here, Lips."

I raise one of my eyebrows in a "what the fuck?" move. She huffs and takes a seat next to Vienna. North and Kray each take an armrest right next to their old ladies. For others it might seem weird for me to talk to them both because it concerns Liah and she should be the one to call her mother but these four are like one solid front.

If Liah would have called the way she called me earlier tonight? These four would be on a plane and dragging her home. The two old ladies would be sobbing and coddling her and those two old bikers would be barking down Archer's neck to find out what the fuck happened. Liah doesn't need that shit right now. She's been struggling with her own mindset and it's a blow to the ego that this happened.

"First…no one died." I shrug. "Well, not that I know of."

"Just get to the fucking point," North grumbles.

I lock my gaze with Vienna. "Liah was shot during an assignment. She's okay. They had to surgically remove the bullet and from what she told me they are not sure if she will regain full function of her arm."

Vienna dashes up and has her fingers covering her mouth as she mumbles, "No. No. This can't be. You're wrong. Shit. You wouldn't be here otherwise. We need to go. I have to go. She needs me. We have to get her."

Kray takes her into his arms. "We will. We'll leave right now and–"

"Yeah, about that…it's not going to happen. She's still recovering and wanted me to let you know she will return home but not until she's managed to scratch the pieces of her self-esteem back together. Not exactly her words but it took a lot for her to follow her own dreams and now this shit happened. So, I'm going to talk with Archer and get things going involving the incident during the mission. Then I'm also going to contact a chapter that's near who can put two brothers on her just to make sure we have eyes on her for our peace of mind. Then I'm going to talk to her tomorrow morning about concrete flight arrangements to bring her home." I connect my gaze with Vienna and firmly state, "She is coming home."

"I don't understand why she didn't call me," Vienna sobs. "I want to hold and comfort her so badly it hurts."

Kray rubs his chin over the crown of his old lady's head while he stares at me. I can clearly see he knows damn well why his daughter contacted me.

It's for this reason I throw it out there, "Your baby is trying to hold tight. Be the fierce lady you raised. She can't do that if we all break down. Now, we're all going to make sure we keep her here when she gets her ass home, okay?"

Vienna bobs her head and her voice is stronger when she says, "Damn right."

"Reva, North, can you walk me out?" I question and step closer to Vienna to grab her in a hug and tell her, "Your girl is fucking strong to reach out to me to get things in place. She doesn't want you two upset and on the road. She wants you right here where her ass wants to be as well. Sit tight and you'll have her home before you know it."

"Thank you." She gives a firm squeeze before seeking the comforting arms of her old man once again.

I head out to my SUV and hear North and Reva both following me out, the gravel crunching under our boots.

"Is she really okay?" Reva questions.

I give her a tight nod. "She sounded defeated but I'm sure it's more about the fact that her dream has been shattered by that bullet that hit her arm. Her future is unsure in her eyes while we damn well know it opens up opportunities you never knew existed until shit happens. Tomorrow morning I'm going to explain to Louie and Luke that their sister is coming home. I also think it might be best if she gets a room at the clubhouse with all the youngsters. You don't want to bring her here and isolate her from the rest."

Reva and North share a look and they know I'm right.

"It's going to be a pain to explain that one to my sister," Reva mutters.

"We got this. There's a reason Liah moved away to do this on her own. We can't clip the wings of our kids; we need to let them catch the wind so they can reach sky-fucking-high. How high or how long they stay up there is fine, but they have to leave the nest and not return. Visit? Sure. But especially Liah needs to have her own space."

"Lips is right," North says to Reva who is now the one bobbing her head.

"We have your back the way you have Liah's," Reva states. "Let us know what you need."

I slip behind the wheel and tell them, "I'll call

tomorrow when I have made some arrangements."

North pats the hood of my SUV. "Drive safe."

"Always," I grunt and head back to the clubhouse.

I'm dead on my feet when I get home. Deeds is still sleeping on the couch and I remove my boots before I quickly dash into the bedroom to take a shower and change into a tank top and boy shorts. Grabbing my phone, I make a quick call to Archer.

My son is still awake and in his office and tells me he will arrange for two brothers to keep an eye on her, making sure she doesn't see them. He also informs me he will gather the information and handle the investigation himself concerning Liah getting shot.

When I know everything is handled for tonight I decide to slip into bed and take my laptop with me. I'll dive into the case tomorrow but for now, I'm going to do a little research to see if I can get some information on Lou's biological father.

The things I find out with a few keystrokes are

concerning and not what I expected. Dammit. As if I didn't have enough shit to handle, I get this twisted insanity landing right in my lap. I shut down the laptop and kill the lights.

Though, sleep doesn't come as easily when all I do is think and stress about all the craziness I discovered just now, Liah's call on top of it, the case I'm handling and everything else I have to handle and deal with.

CHAPTER SIX

DEEDS

I rub the back of my neck as I saunter into the living room. It's early morning and I've had the best sleep I've had in forever. It didn't matter that I woke up on the couch in the middle of the night and moved into the bedroom to fall right back to sleep holding my woman.

She wasn't there when I woke up a few minutes ago and after I washed up and got dressed I went looking for her. She's sitting at the table staring at her notepad. There's a frown on her face and she's nibbling on her bottom lip. I'm fairly sure she's missing the snakebite piercings she usually wears and nibbles on.

"What's bugging you, love?" I question and lean on the table.

Her eyes find mine. "Can I run something by you?"

I grab the back of the chair and drag it away from the table to take a seat. "You know there's no need to ask. Fire away, I'm all yours, all ears, always."

She releases a deep sigh. "The diner I like to keep to myself? The one you were waiting in front of yesterday when you came looking for me?"

I give her a nod.

"The coffee is amazing and so are all the things she bakes. Lou…Alouette Perry, she inherited that diner when her mother passed away. I've been going to that place for about a year now. One day Lou asked me what I did for a living and I told her I'm somewhat of a private investigator. Yesterday Lou asked if she could hire me to find her biological father. I fucking did. Found out yesterday who he is… well, somewhat. Dammit. Lou is a sweet girl, a hard worker, and definitely a tough woman who has her feet planted firmly on the ground."

"Okay," I rumble. "Why am I getting the feeling you're building up to ripping the rug out from under her feet?"

"Because I fucking am," Lynn snaps. "And I hate it. I don't know if I should tell her, keep it to myself, or blow shit wide open so it will also affect a club brother."

I lean forward and place my forearms on the table. "What the fuck? What does a club brother have to do with your Lou from the diner?"

"Because," she says in a duh tone of voice. "Rack is her…brother."

I let myself drop back into the chair. "You mean… shit. Are you sure? If Rack is her brother then her father is in jail for first-degree murder."

"No. I mean yes. I mean…I don't know," Lips seethes and jolts to her feet to start pacing. She's rubbing her left arm when she starts to ramble, "Rack mentioned his parents broke up a few weeks before his father murdered a man. He was six years old at the time. He was placed in foster care because they couldn't track down his mother. He never went looking for her because he feels she walked out on him. Well, when Lou asked me to find her biological father I had a first name, a street name, and some other details and it led me to Rack's father. Now here comes the twisted fuck-up. The man Rack's father killed? I went through his file and saw a picture of the fucker...Lou has some similarities. The fucker Rack's father killed was a rapist. A rapist!" She whirls around to face me, eyes blazing she says, "I think Rack's mother was raped."

"Holy fuck," I mutter. "If what you're saying is true then Lou is the kid of a rapist and Rack's father killed the man who raped his woman."

"They were business partners. The homicide detectives on the case over two decades ago simply thought they had a dispute and he killed his business partner in cold blood." Lips rubs her sternum and takes a few deep breaths. "I'm thinking the man saw his whole family fall apart. His woman being raped by his partner, maybe she broke down because she left the country. I checked. It's why the authorities couldn't find her when they were searching for a relative to take Rack. She wasn't registered anywhere. I know Lou told me the first ten years of her life her mom and her lived in Australia, Europe, Canada, everywhere and nowhere until they came here five years ago and bought the diner. Dammit to hell and back. What am I going to do? I can't tell her, can I? I sure as fuck can't tell Rack. She has no one. This is gonna hit hard."

I get to my feet and take her into my arms. "Hey now, she has you," I murmur and she leans into me.

My fingers side into her hair and I fist the gray silk to angle her head back to take her mouth. Letting my tongue slide over her bottom lip, I tease her to give me access to her wicked lips. She opens and I get to deepen our kiss.

Her fingers sneak under my shirt, nails raking over my skin and I'm completely under her spell. She rips her mouth from mine and places her forehead on my chest. Confusion hits me why she would break a damn good kiss but the way she's heaving and has her fist buried into my leather cut lets me know something is wrong.

"Hey, love," I croak and cup her face to I can see her. "What's wrong?"

"My chest." She winces and stumbles back.

I scoop her into my arms and place her on the couch.

"I'll get Depay," I tell her and turn but stop dead in my tracks when she grabs my leather cut again.

"Don't you dare," she threatens. "I'm perfectly fine. I'm just getting all worked up."

I narrow my eyes as I stare down at her. "You were rubbing your sternum earlier and your left arm. What if you're having a fucking heart attack? I'm not losing you, dammit."

"Fine, then call Ivy," she snaps and I'm already palming my phone to make the call.

Luckily Ivy is here within a few minutes, two medical bags in hand, and squats down in front of Lips. I give her a rundown of what I saw while Lips glares at me. I don't fucking care. I want to know what's wrong.

Ivy hooks Lips onto a portable ECG machine. We

have loads of medical equipment with the high-risk cases we're always working on. Every damn second can matter when saving lives and it's why a few brothers are EMTs. Ivy here being an ER surgeon it's as close to getting Lips to the hospital as we can get.

Damn that stubborn woman. My own stress level is rising and I'm pacing the room waiting for Ivy to tell me what she thinks is going on. I've bitten my lip more than once before I can't take it anymore.

"And? Is she having a heart attack? Should we go to the hospital?" I ask through gritted teeth.

Ivy is done studying the ECG and is shaking her head. "No. Everything tells me you had a panic attack."

"See?" Lips snaps. "Nothing wrong."

"Well," Ivy starts but Lips shakes her head.

"I just got all worked up. I'm fine. Get these things off me and I'll have some more coffee so you two can stop worrying."

Ivy removes the sensors from Lips' skin and is murmuring under her breath. Lips glares at her but nods to whatever it is she's telling her. Another few minutes later Ivy has gathered her things and I'm walking her out the door.

I glance over my shoulder to make sure Lips is out of earshot when I ask Ivy, "Tell me, did she really have a panic attack? Doesn't she need checkups?"

"Tell him I don't need to go to the hospital," Lips bellows from the living room.

Ivy chuckles. "Nothing gets by her." She gives me a warm smile. "I get the concerns and I would like to run a few more tests and she's agreed to do them later this week when I'm at work. We all know we can't force her into something and I'm sure if you leave the topic alone she will swing by soon enough. She's just as spooked as we are."

I bob my head. "Fine."

"I would say make sure she takes it slow for a couple of days but it's Lips soooo…good luck with that."

"Har fucking har," I grumble and Ivy walks away with a soft chuckle trailing behind her.

I close the door and stride into the living room,

ready for a firm talk with my old lady but as soon as she sees me, she gives me the finger.

"Fuck off. I know everything you're going to tell me so shut it," she grumbles.

"What if this is a test run, huh? The whole panic attack shit? What if your heart does say 'the hell with it,' what then? I refuse to let that happen. Your heart is mine, I own that fucking heartbeat," I seethe in frustration, anger, and fucking fear of losing her.

Her face softens and she steps closer, taking my face in her hands. "I remember you telling me how you own my fucking heartbeat. Gets me all warm and fuzzy." She softly brushes her lips against mine. "I already promised Ivy I would swing by the hospital for a few checks, okay? Besides, it gives me a great excuse to check out the nurses."

I step back and grumble, "For fuck's sake, really? Work? You're diving right back into everything while you have to take it slow?"

Lips places her hands on her hips. "I was going to ask if you could help me out with the shit I'm balancing, but I'd gather by your reaction that you're refusing."

The corner of my mouth twitches. "You wanna work together? Allow me to take some of your load? Let Bee handle the other old ladies and shit that you normally take on without demanding everyone to handle their own shit?"

She narrows her eyes. "I wouldn't go that far but I might have already started delegating when this whole tightness in my chest and tingles in my arm shit started. Besides, Bee is the president's old lady, she's quite capable of handling shit." Lips shrugs. "Gives me the opportunity to pick my fights and the best moments to interfere with everyone."

I step closer and sneak my arm around her waist to pull her against me. "You have?"

She murmurs something and it takes my ears and mind a breath or two to process it and realize she just admitted, "I'm not getting any younger and my body isn't capable the way it used to be."

"You're still fucking perfect in every way, woman," I growl and give her a fierce kiss.

She melts into me but ends it way too fast. "Can

we handle Lou's screwed-up shit first? It's giving me heartburn. I have to get this over with, though I'd rather not but there's no way around it."

"You're right," I agree. "You should let her know exactly what you found out. You can even offer to take a DNA test to make sure. Who knows, Rack's mother might have been pregnant before she was raped. We're all here for her but it's Lou's choice if she wants to tell Rack. Yeah, coming with you might be good to show support. Even if Rack is my club brother, we'll let her know it's her choice."

"Good. I could use some good coffee and a cinnamon caramel muffin." She strolls over to the table and shoves documents into a file. "Maybe we could talk through the other case when we get back. I've made some calls and found out there are two other retirement homes with a death count that isn't normal. I want to cross-check names. Maybe one of the nurses who works at Ivy's hospital also takes on extra shifts or something."

"Smart thinking," I remark. "Walk me through it when we get back so I can check while you get your beauty sleep." She starts to glare at me but I cut off her rambling thoughts by telling her, "Don't give me any shit. I know you haven't been sleeping well."

"Fine," she huffs. "Oh, and I might as well tell you right now before anyone else tells you…Liah called me last night. She was on an assignment when someone shot her in the arm. They removed the bullet but the surgeon can't promise full function in her arm so her dream has blown to shit."

Fucking hell, poor girl. "She called you for damage control?"

"Yeah. I went over to Kray and North to make sure they knew what happened and to tell them to stay put. She's coming home but needs time to process everything. I also asked Archer to look into the incident to see if we can find out who fucking shot her."

I can tell her anger is spiking again and I pull her into my arms. "Sounds like you handled everything and delegated perfectly. Exactly what Liah needed and why everyone throws everything your way."

I know it's useless to tell her she needs to take

a step back. Lips will always be the way she is and can handle everything flawlessly, but everyone has their limit of bullshit before steam starts to come out of their ears.

With everything thrown her way, it's normal to feel swamped and it makes some of my worries fade. At least it's a big win for her to ask me to help her. It's a start to not only make sure to lighten her load but also for spending more time together; a win-win for both of us.

CHAPTER SEVEN

LYNN

"I know it's a lot to take in," I tell Lou and reach across the table to cover her hand with mine. "Just let me know what you want or need, and we'll make it happen."

"We all will," Deeds states from beside me.

Lou is still wearing a stunned look filled with disbelief. "I...I don't know. I have to process all of it, but my first instinct is to do the DNA test to make sure if Rack is related. From what you guys have told and shown me I'm kinda hoping for a miracle and that he's my full brother instead of half. Because... shit." Her voice breaks and I can tell her eyes are stinging with tears when she's blinking a few times.

I give her hand another squeeze. "Anything you need, chickie. Just take your time."

"Thank you," she croaks and glances around the diner. "I need to work. It's a good distraction."

"Ain't that the truth? I'm always keeping myself busy from my rambling thoughts and pains my body holds. I don't think I could function if I didn't work. Pretty sure I'd be dust in the wind if they cut me off," I admit, realizing only now it's one of my flaws to handle everything myself but at the same time it's something I can't do without.

I feel Deeds' hand on my knee. "It's why she asked me to help her out. I'm glad too. First, I thought taking work out of her hands would make her take it slow but I was wrong. My old lady is like the big fucking spider in the Broken Deeds MC web. Always aware of every pull on the strings and there in a flash to jump into action. The one everyone knows is there even if you can't see her." He shoots me a grin. "The one every-fucking-one is afraid of 'cause she's as fierce and ruthless as they come. It also makes her strong enough to reach out when she wants to lean on me. Fucking great 'cause helping her means we get to spend more time together and still get shit done. Way better. Point is, you're also not alone in all of this. The information my old lady gathered or not, you're already a part of us. Lips considers you a friend so we're all here for you no matter what. Which also means I get to bring her here each morning to have breakfast together now that she finally decided to share this place with me. Damn these pancakes are seriously fucking delicious."

The whole spider statement gives me the damn creeps and reminds me of a time when Deeds and I were first together. His grandmother had this huge mother-of-all-spiders in her house and she caught it with a glass and added some tape on the top. Only to shove it away on a shelf in a shed out back along with a collection of glasses, each holding another damn spider.

Quickly shoving the memory away, I take Deeds' hand off my knee and wrap both of mine around his.

"Sometimes the reminder of what's right in front of you is enough to give you the necessary boost to pull through the shit you're dealing with."

"Damn right," Deeds muses and leans in to brush a kiss against the corner of my mouth.

"Thank you. It's a lot to process but at the same time, it warms my heart to know I have friends to fall back on. This diner is all I have and it eats away at my social life. It might seem like a lot of customers are friends but at the end of the day I'm all alone." Lou gives me a sad smile. "I sold the house after my mother died. It didn't feel right to stay there all alone and by selling it I could wipe away the debts we had. The small, one-bedroom apartment above the diner is enough for me."

"Like we mentioned, we're here for whatever you need," Deeds repeats.

"The DNA test," she firmly states.

I'm thankful she's taking this step and thank fuck she hasn't met Rack yet. My bestie, Blue, had a similar issue when a dude she met wanted her, only to realize they were related. Yeah, talk about awkwardness but thank fuck because my brother isn't the sharing kind and would have killed anyone who tried to steal his woman.

Deeds reaches inside his leather cut and pulls out an oral swab kit. Handing the box to Lou he tells her, "Take the swab out and rub it against the inside of your cheek. We have our own DNA lab and will have the results in a few days."

She takes the swab and does as instructed before handing it back. "Thank you."

Deeds dips his chin and Lou wanders off to help the waitress to fill out the orders.

"She's good people," Deeds murmurs and his words make me smile.

"She is. I've been around her for a while now. Very observant, helpful, driven, determined, fierce… I like her."

Deeds glances at me and states, "Coffee and baked goods aren't the only reason you come back here."

I slowly shake my head and let my eyes find Lou. "No. I've been coming here since her mother was running it along with Lou. Little chitchats brought up the discussion where Lou's mother asked me to look after her daughter just in case something would happen to her. There was no need for her to mention it; I would have done it either way. I just feel…I don't know."

"A bit protective like the momma bear you are," Deeds murmurs. "Understandable with most of our daughters living far away. Not that Lou is in any way a substitute, but the girl clearly longs for a personal connection even if she's always making fucking connections here in this diner. Like she said, at the end of the day she's all alone. Knowing her, even if it's for a small moment and through what you've told me about her, I'm not liking her feeling all alone one damn bit."

I shoot him a grin, my heart warming due to his words. "She got to you too, didn't she?"

"Yeah," he rumbles. "And I hope to fuck this swab tells us Rack is her full brother. Either way, it won't matter."

"No, it won't. She'll have us either way," I agree.

We finish our coffee and head back to the clubhouse. I'm on the back of Deeds' bike and it's been a while. There's always something that requires us to either take the SUV or handle things separately.

In the past, we would go for a ride just for the sake of enjoying the ride. Life flashes by just like the scenery and you just go through life living it. What you should do is simply take a breath and enjoy your surroundings and the damn moment.

I take in a breath, filling my lungs with the much-needed oxygen but with it, I fill my heart with the reminder of all the good my life is surrounded with. My old man, whom my arms are wrapped tight around, for instance.

The man might be an overbearing asshole with a dash of insensitivity and a truckload of annoyance he brings out with his actions but at the end of the night? He's my overbearing asshole. The one who steps up to fight any battle to win it for me, even if he has to fight me head-on to make me aware of how much I need to value myself along with it.

I give him a little squeeze and my heart fucking

flutters when he places his hand on my thigh and gives a squeeze, keeping it in place for a few breaths before grabbing the handlebar again. Yeah, our love is fierce, dedicated, and fucking invincible.

Deeds plants his boots firmly on the ground and balances the bike while I step off. I grab my purse and shove my hand in there to search for the keys. My old man chuckles and unclips the house key from the rest of his keys and hands it over.

"I'm gonna drop off the swab myself at the lab so there's no delay," he rumbles. "Are you going to dive into the names of those nurses?"

I purse my lips. "I'm going to call Liah first to check how she's doing and after that call Vienna. Then I'll check the names."

"Take your time making sure your ladies are fine. Gives me the time to ride back and forth so we can go over that list together and talk shit through once we're done."

Leaning in I brush my lips against his. "Then you better hurry back or I'm gonna start without you."

I'm about to pull back but the man's hand flashes

out to bury his fist in my hair. He takes my mouth in a fierce kiss that has me rubbing my legs together to soothe the ache he's creating inside my pussy.

Pulling back, he growls, "I don't mind you starting without me as long as you don't finger-fuck yourself to an orgasm."

I take a step in the direction of the house when I tell him with a load of sass, "I'm not making any promises."

I swear I hear him growl over the rumbling of his bike as he peels out of the driveway. My belly flops like a lovestruck teenager as I watch him ride off before I enter the house. My mind, body, and damn soul feels better. Lighter by leaning on my old man while simultaneously getting the old spark back that was always simmering on the back burner.

Life pushes you along, dragging you through the dust and letting it settle so you'll lose your shine. Thank fuck my man still sees my worth and rubbed me the right way to get my glow back 'cause I feel damn fine.

I throw my purse on the couch and head for the

kitchen to grab a bottle of water. Pulling my phone from my pocket I tap the screen and search for Liah's number. After rambling back and forth for a few minutes we end the call. Even if she's still struggling with healing and the turn of events, she is looking forward to coming home.

Liah asked her mother if she could arrange a plane ticket for next week and I'm glad she gave Vienna a chance to arrange for her girl to come home. I know all too well it's hard to deal with failure, especially when it comes to family.

I make a quick call to Vienna and let her rattle about her girl and when she's coming home. My ear is warm and red from the two calls, but I can't help but make another one to Blue and catch up on her and my brother.

We're not supposed to discuss club business but I'm too nosy not to demand an answer. I could hear my brother talking in the back to let Blue know it's okay to let me know that my brother stepped back as the president of Areion Fury MC.

I'm glad the twins took over and it might be

weird to have two presidents in one chapter but those two practically share a brain. Each president runs a club their own way and so does the next generation. Besides, Blue and my brother deserve to have more time and less stress. Hell, the last few days have shown me as much.

A smile tugs my face when I'm gathering the things I need to dive back into the case. Deeds offered to help me and in return, I'm waiting for him to come home instead of handling it myself. I'm actually looking forward to it so I can tease him some more.

Fingers crossed we'll end up fucking on the table. Uncomfortable, backbreaking, but it'll make us feel more alive for sure. I'm booting up the laptop when I hear the rumble of a bike. A few minutes later Deeds is striding into the living room.

A slow smile slides across his face and I swear my pussy starts to tingle. We might be older, crazier, and not as fast as we used to be, but damn if we'll stop living life to the fullest. Especially now that we've cleared some mental dust bunnies, adjusted our course, and are both hellbent on spending more time together. Either working, talking, or letting our bodies handle the communication.

I'm definitely looking forward to the last part. Though first we need to get some work done and it will grant me the opportunity to get him all worked up, tease the hell out of him, so the man will ravish me when it's time to hit the sheets.

Screw panic attacks. Screw taking it easy. I want my body aching in a different way; first with the need to be filled, which will later be replaced by feeling sore. Yeah. Best. Plan. Ever.

CHAPTER EIGHT
Five days later

DEEDS

"Something wrong?" Lochlan questions.

North and Kray both glance over their shoulder at me as I move through the main room of the clubhouse while trying to give my cock as less friction as fucking possible.

"Don't think I've seen you wear sweatpants into the clubhouse for a long time there, brother." Kray chuckles. "Like Lochlan asked...what the fuck is going on with the lower half of your body. It's like you're walking with cracked eggs in your underwear."

I ignore them and take a seat.

"Stop harassing the fucker. Y'all should be jealous instead of nagging him," Ramrod quips.

I lift my chin in a silent thanks to Broke who slides a mug filled with black coffee in front of me.

"And why is that? You know something we don't?" Depay asks.

Ramrod shrugs. "It takes one to know one, I guess."

"What the fuck is that supposed to mean?" Lochlan grumbles.

North throws his head back and laughs.

I ignore everyone, or at least I try to until Ramrod says, "Pussy burn. It's obvious by the way he's walking; the man overused his cock."

Everyone falls silent and I can feel their stare. My phone vibrates with an incoming message and I try to focus on that when I see Rack stepping behind the bar.

"That's something to fucking strive for you assholes," Rack states. "Us young fuckers can only hope we find an old lady like Lips. Fierce, loyal, and still consumed with her old man."

I'm grinning like a damn loon hearing the compliment as I open my email. The DNA results are in and I hold my breath when I read the results, hoping Rack is Lou's full brother instead of half. Holy fuck, I have to show Lips the results.

I jump from my seat and instantly regret the move. My cock feels as if I've rubbed it on the damn asphalt. Like fuck will I regret overusing it and trying some old moves but I guess taking it slow the next few days is a damn necessity.

Judging from the way my woman is still sleeping in bed at ten this morning I'd say she'd be fine with the suggestion. Though, it's like we're both caught in a new lust drive where we don't fuck for the sake of fucking or getting off but it's the spark in our veins that adds something special.

"Rack," I snap. "You're coming with me."

I turn on my heel and head out of the clubhouse in the direction of my home. The crunching of gravel behind me lets me know Rack is following me. The scent of fresh coffee assaults my nose when I enter the house and my feet automatically carry me into the kitchen.

Lips is leaning against the kitchen counter and has her hands wrapped around a mug, taking a sip as her eyes land on mine. I reach for my phone and tap the screen to pull up the email I just received before I turn the device her way.

She takes in the information and mutters, "Holy fuck."

Placing her mug on the counter she launches herself at me and I have to take a step back to brace myself. Fucking hell, feeling her curves melt against me makes lust spike in my veins. See? It's like we've turned into horny teenagers. I bury my head into the crook of her neck and breathe her in before I slowly plant her feet back on the ground.

"Wanna head over and show it to her?" I question and throw my thumb over my shoulder to add in a low voice, "I say we take the kid with us. It will stay her choice to tell him or not but seeing him might be a good motivation to break any tension or doubt she might have."

Lips bites her bottom lip, clearly missing her

snake bite piercings she always plays with. "I guess you're right. Sure. Why not? But you're going to tell him not to share the diner or mention how fucking good her food is with anyone else."

I bark out a laugh and sneak my arm around her waist to pull her close and murmur in her ear, "You got it, sexy momma."

"Keep the sweet talk to yourself. My pussy needs a break and if you keep smiling, feeling, and talking the way you do we'll end up fucking again."

Chuckling I admit, "We definitely need to give both cock and pussy a break."

"Well, let's head over to Lou and tell her the news and get some breakfast. Then I hope Bee has the results for me so we can work on my case," Lips suggests.

A few days ago, Lips cross-checked the names of nurses to see if one works at both the hospital and the retirement homes unexplained deaths occurred in. Sadly, there wasn't a hit but Lips knew Bee had a way to check if family or people who share addresses work at similar places and has asked to do an extended search.

There hasn't been another unexplained death till now but time is a pressing matter. Not to mention, we need to find the one who killed the others because Lips was able to prove by running another check that they have used insulin. The almost perfect murder because it's not a test they use on a normal autopsy.

"Sounds like a plan. Let's take the SUV," I suggest, knowing Vachs is still working on my bike to add a little something he mentioned to me yesterday.

Lips grins. "We sure need the space between our bodies."

I chuckle and hold out my hand. She laces her fingers with mine and I place a kiss on the top of her hand as I murmur, "We can eat each other up and know how to pace ourselves, love. We're not the horny teenagers we seemed to be the past few days."

I guide her out of the kitchen and point at the door when Rack glances up from checking his phone while he was waiting in the living room.

"We're heading out to get some breakfast and you're coming with us," I tell him and Lips squeezes my hand. "Oh, and that reminds me. Not a word to anyone else about this place because we want to keep it to ourselves. The food and company is damn good so be respectful and polite, get me?"

"Sure thing," he grunts.

"Are you joining us in the cage or are you taking your bike?" Lips asks as we walk out to the SUV.

"No cage," Rack grunts and jogs off toward the clubhouse to go around it to the front where his bike is parked.

"Liah is coming home tomorrow," Lips quips once we're on the road.

I give her a slight nod. "Luke and Louie mentioned it last night. Those two are picking her up from the airport."

"Did they make sure to have a room ready at the clubhouse?" she questions.

"Vienna and Kray wanted to bring her home," I start and I can practically feel the temperature in the small space rise a few degrees so I quickly add, "But Luke and Louie told their parents she's staying with them for the first couple of days and that she gets to decide where to stay after that."

Lips rubs her sternum and I hate seeing her getting all worked up again. The past few days have been better stress related but I know damn well panic attacks aren't simply over when you know what it is and relax. The mind and body are complicated.

I reach out and take her hand, brush my mouth against her knuckles and place our joined hands on my thigh as I drive to the diner. A while later I turn into the parking lot and Rack parks his bike beside our SUV. We all stroll into the diner.

There are a few customers enjoying a late breakfast. Lou spots us as soon as we stroll inside. She's behind the counter serving a customer. Lips asks for my phone and I hand it to her as I place my hand on Rack's shoulder and steer him to a table in the back.

"You guys come here a lot?" Rack asks as he takes a seat in the booth across from me.

I give a curt shake with my head. "Nah, me just recently. It's Lips' secret hideaway where she gets to enjoy her coffee and baked goodness without the shit going on in her own world. She's been coming here a long time and has become friends with the woman who used to own it and her daughter. The woman asked her to keep an eye out if something happened to her and when she passed away Lips… well, you know how she is."

The corner of Rack's mouth twitches. "She made her extended family."

Damn. Close to the truth and it's a shame Rack doesn't know what we found out these past few days. He might even look at his own father differently if he knew all the details. He was young when this shit happened and being in foster care made him distance himself from his father and never so much as looked for or asked about his mother.

Lips strolls our way and takes a seat next to me. Lou steps closer and is eying Rack. I'm pretty sure my woman showed her the results of the DNA test and it's up to Lou to decide what to do with the information. Fucking hell, I want nothing more than to tell Rack myself but it's not my place.

"Can I have a coffee and a blueberry muffin?" I question when I see Lou grabbing her notepad.

"Sure thing," she quips and glances at Lips. "The usual for you?"

"Heck yes." Lips grins.

Lou turns to Rack and the guy's jaw hits the table when he sees Lou for the first time. A stunned look slides over his face with his eyes bulging before he turns as white as a sheet. It's as if the fucker saw a ghost.

"You said you didn't tell him anything," Lou grumbles under her breath.

"We didn't," Lips assures her.

Rack shakes his head as if to clear it when he says, "Sorry. It's just that…you're the spitting image of my mother." His cheeks flush and he mutters, "I need some air. Excuse me."

He's about to get to his feet but Lou blocks him.

Rack stares up at her when she says, "I asked Lips to find my biological father. She came here today to give me the results. They left it up to me to decide if I share it with anyone but seeing you're here, mentioning how I look like our mother…how can I not?" Lou turns to face me. "Can you show him the email?"

I reach for my phone and tap the screen a few times before I place it on the table in front of Rack. He slides his finger over the screen, quickly reading over the information in the email. He leans back and stares at us. Lou points at the seat next to Rack.

"May I?" she asks and Rack nods.

A few minutes of silence pass before Lou says, "I was shocked when Lips told me my biological father might be a rapist and that the man my mother loved killed him and ended up in jail. I never imagined something as screwed-up as this would be tied to my past and deep down, I hoped there was a tiny miracle that could undo the chance of my biological father being a criminal. Yet…seeing the results…knowing my biological father is in prison…the why and how somehow soothes an open wound while it doesn't take away my sadness and disbelief. To be honest? I have no clue how to handle it all. I wasn't going to say anything to anyone and process everything myself first but seeing you, hearing you say I'm the spitting image of your mother? My mother?" Her voice wavers and tears spill over her cheeks.

I hear soft sniffling beside me and I wrap my arm around Lips to pull her close. Fucking hell, even my throat clogs up with the kind of emotion that's thickening the air around us.

"You're my sister," Rack states with a load of disbelief. "My full-fucking-blood sister."

Lou's head bobs and she says in a soft voice, "I thought I was all alone. No family left. And now? I have a brother." She bites her lips and shyly murmurs, "Well, if you want to get to know me that is."

"Want?" Rack snaps and before anyone can say or do anything he reaches out and grabs her in a bear hug. "You're my fucking sister. You don't have a damn choice, sis. You have me whether you want me or not. Fucking hell." He pulls her back and lets his eyes suck in every detail of her face. "A sister." His head turns our way and he's wearing a shit-eating grin when he says, "I have a fucking sister."

Lips quickly wipes her eyes with the back of her hand and clears her throat before she says, "Hell yeah, you do."

His eyes suddenly narrow and his whole face becomes serious when he snaps, "We need to keep this place to ourselves. I don't want any of the brothers coming here. Fucking hell. I have a sister. What if she spikes the interest of one of my brothers? Yeah, not going to happen."

My head falls back and I bark out a laugh but it abruptly ends when Lynn jabs her elbow into my side.

"Stop laughing," Lips grumbles.

She turns her attention to Rack and I now notice Lou is glaring at him.

"You heard me before we came here but that just means I want to keep this place my peaceful getaway and not to keep cocks away from your sister. She has a life and her own decisions. Shit, dude. You've know you were her brother for like three minutes and thirty-nine seconds and you're acting like a cock-block Neanderthal."

Lou chuckles at Lips' words and reaches across the table to give her hand a squeeze. "Thanks, Lynn. Appreciate it. Now. I have to get to work."

She shoots a quick look over her shoulder to the counter where the waitress is having a hard time filling the orders by herself.

"I'll get your order over in a jiffy. And Rack? Is it okay if we exchange numbers or agree to meet sometime for coffee or dinner or whatever? I'd love to talk or show you pictures or discuss where we go from here."

He gives her a warm smile. "I'm not leaving here until we've exchanged numbers and talked some more. I have all the fucking time in the world so I'll be right here."

She returns the smile and I hear Lips sigh in happiness. This is also what Broken Deeds stands for; it's not just the whole 'justice will be done' part working for the government gives us. We sometimes work missing-person cases and handle personal shit as a favor.

Brotherhood, family, loyalty, and having each other's backs throughout the ups and downs life drags us through. The fact that Lips was drawn to this place, kept coming here, and in the end, was able to give Lou a piece of her missing family is as if it was meant to be.

Call it a miracle how Lou wasn't born out of rape and damned circumstances drove a happy family apart. Decades later brother and sister are reunited. Treasured moments makes you aware of the warmth and strength hearts are capable of.

Hope. Love. Life. Connection of those dots gives you the bull's-eye of a future you're aiming for. At least I do with my partner in crime right beside me every step of the way. I glance at Lips and lean in to give her a kiss, tasting the promise of what lies ahead on her wicked tongue.

Pussy-burned cock be damned.

CHAPTER NINE

LYNN

I cover my mouth with one hand to stifle a yawn while grabbing the mug filled with coffee in the other as I wander back to the couch. I wanted to dive into the information Bee was gathering for me by cross-checking addresses from nurses from the hospital and nursing homes yesterday but something came up and Bee couldn't get it in time.

The text I woke up to twenty minutes ago let me know the information is in my mailbox and it's why I've made myself some coffee. Shit. I wish I could go back to Lou and have a nice caramel cinnamon muffin along with it.

Releasing a deep sigh, I sink down into the couch and take a few sips of coffee before I reach for the laptop and boot the thing up. Deeds is still sleeping. He mentioned Archer wanted to talk to him in church at eleven so he's allowed to sleep in.

I wish I was still in bed snoring but I had a shitty night. I had to pee at three AM and couldn't get back to sleep until five, only to be wide awake at seven, tossing and turning until my phone vibrated with a text. I decided to give up on sleep and might as well get to work.

Grabbing my glasses, I open the document and start to scroll through the information. Hot damn, I knew I was right. Well, at first I thought it was one nurse who was giving patients an overdose of insulin but it seems there's one address connected to both the hospital and two retirement homes.

My phone starts to ring and I reach for the thing, noticing it's Lou calling me and cheerfully quip, "Hey, Lou."

"Lynn." The way she impatiently sighs out my name makes me straighten my spine.

"Everything okay?" I question.

Lou is quiet for a heartbeat or two–and my heart is beating way fucking fast–before she says, "I think it's best if you don't come around for a while."

My chest squeezes painfully as confusion hits me just as hard. "What? Why?"

"It's overwhelming, to say the least. I'm trying to get used to the idea of everything but I feel extremely crowded. I need space and time. Will you let Rack know he needs to respect my wishes? I explained it to him yesterday, and again this morning, but I don't think he's getting the hint, nor the threats I threw at his head." Another deep sigh rips from her. "I like you a lot Lynn and I'm sorry to ask this but seeing you also means being confronted with everything and I wasn't prepared to have an…never mind. Just…give me time, okay?"

I don't have fucking time to say something because she hangs up. Anger flares inside my veins and I jolt up. My arm is killing me, my hand along with it and my chest feels so damn tight. Shoving everything to the background, I snatch my keys from the table and shove my phone into the back pocket of my jeans.

I exchange my fluffy socks with my biker boots and stomp out the door, heading straight to the clubhouse. That motherfucker Rack. I'm pretty damn sure the overbearing Neanderthal did something to make her feel as if she's trapped in a corner with nowhere to go.

"Rack," I bellow as soon as I step into the clubhouse.

It's all I manage when my chest feels like a truck just hit me full frontal. I can't breathe. I reach for my chest but my fucking hand tingles and feels as if I'm unable to control it. What the fuck is happening? Bee appears in my vision that's starting to taint with spots.

"Lips? What's going on? Are you okay? Shit. Come on. Ivy is at the hospital. She told me about last time and warned me to bring you to her if something happened and this is something fucking happening." Bee sneaks her arm around my waist and lets me lean on her while we stumble our way through the clubhouse.

She helps me into her car and runs around the thing to get behind the wheel. It looks like she's firing off a message on her phone and I close my eyes, I try to get a grip on myself. I'm only having a panic attack, right? Not a damn heart attack. Fucking hell, sure feels like it.

No. No. Fucking. Way. Am I going to sneak out on life itself this way? I have so much to live for. Shoving my boot up Rack's ass for one. Drinking more coffee, riding on the back of my old man's bike, fucking so my pussy is sore for days. Dammit. I can think up a million more things.

They say life flashes before your eyes when you die. Well, all good things are on repeat and I want a re-run and add-ons so fuck you, death. I'm not going out this way. I feel like I'm hyperventilating and not getting enough oxygen into my body.

Shit turns black for a moment and then Bee is suddenly in my face.

"Are you okay?" she questions with a load of worry.

I grit my teeth and snap, "No, I'm not fucking okay. Apparently, my body thinks it's fucking funny to panic or some shit whenever I get too damn angry."

"Worked up," Ivy quips from beside Bee. "You get worked up and trigger a panic attack. Come on, let's get you inside so I can run a few tests to make sure everything is okay."

It's so damn frustrating to practically lose a grip on my own damn body. I raise my eyebrow in the direction of the wheelchair Ivy brought and the woman chuckles.

Ivy shrugs. "Hey, it was worth a shot, old woman."

"Old woman?" I snap. "That's old lady to you, bitch."

Bee chuckles and mutters to Ivy, "You might as well admit you called her old man and that he's on his way."

"What the fuck you two?" I grumble. "I'm totally fine, I just need to get a handle on the backlash when I get fucking pissed. That reminds me, I'm gonna get my fingers around Rack's throat and strangle the fucker."

"What did that asshole do to upset you?" Deeds enters my vision and swoops me off my damn feet as he starts to carry me into the emergency room. "Where do you need her, Ivy?"

I should be pissed but at the same time, I'm completely drained and find myself snuggling against my man's chest. Ivy wanted me to swing by to run a few checks and I should have done it right after I had my first panic attack. So, I might as well let her use me as a pin cushion and turn me inside out to see if something other than the panic attack is throwing me back on my ass.

Deeds chuckles and tightens his arms. "I think she's gonna take a nap on my lap while you draw blood and whatever else you need to do."

"Physically it takes a lot from your body," Ivy starts and I zone out, inhaling Deeds' scent calms me down.

A little while later I've had Ivy poke and prod me and turn me inside out with scans, and other shit.

I'm getting ready to get the fuck out of here when a young nurse strides into my room. She gives my man a seductive smile, and that move isn't the only reason the hairs on the back of my neck stand on end.

I recognize her from the picture in her work file, the one I was checking when I noticed the address check Bee did for me. Ruby. Ruby Fenlowe, my number one suspect. Her sister, Nance, works in a retirement home.

Before everything went to shit this morning, I was going to get a thorough background check on both of them. Fucking hell. Now I'm lying in a damn hospital bed with an angel of death shooting "fuck me" eyes in my husband's direction.

"He's married and his cock has a red rash from fucking me too damn much. So, don't even think about flirting or I'll grab that plastic spoon over there and scoop your fucking eyes out before I shove them up your ass like damn anal beads," I snarl.

My chest is rising and falling and it's causing my breathing to go haywire again. Dammit. Not again. Not fucking now. I recognize the surge of mixed shit triggering my body to hop right into a panic attack.

I have to cool my tits, especially with this nurse hanging around me. I can't flat-out tell Deeds this is our number one suspect; we have to do more research to nail this one and her sister along with it.

"Hotlips," Deeds murmurs as his strong, big hands cup my face, making our gaze connect.

This man. My fucking beacon through havoc, mayhem, bearing children, raising those little shits, and after decades of living together, he still manages to warm my heart and soul to be the serenity I need when I want to raise hell and spit fire.

"There she is," he rumbles with a sexy smile.

"Keep smiling like that and you'll be the one lying in this bed with a bandaged cock," I mutter and the man barks out a laugh.

"Great, sounds like you're ready to get out of here," Ivy states with a load of laughter in her voice. "Oh, hey, Ruby. Did your shift start already? Damn, look at the time." Ivy chuckles. "My shift ended over an hour ago. Well then. Ruby, can you get Lynn's discharge papers?"

The killer nurse sashays out of the room and I turn to Deeds to whisper under my breath, "That cunt is our angel of death prime suspect."

His head rears back and he throws a quick look over his shoulder before connecting our gaze again. "What's the plan?"

Decades of trust forged a strong bond where he instantly knows I'm serious. That and I used the C-word. There is no damn way I'd use the word cunt voluntarily and if someone calls me that they'd better hold onto their balls or tits 'cause I'll be hitting where it hurts the most; that's how much I hate the damn word.

I purse my lips as I think over what to do about Ruby. "I don't know. I was checking the information when Lou called and then I got pissed and went to confront Rack and I ended up here."

"Fuck," Deeds mutters. "Then I guess we're gonna bust you out of here, dive into the information, and come back here. Ivy mentioned her shift just started, right?"

"Smart man." I grin and then realize my unfinished business. "Somewhere in between all of that we need to make time to kick Rack's ass."

"I'm sure we can make it work," he tells me. "Start talking about that fucker, he's the reason another panic attack hit you, right?"

The nurse strolls back in with the paperwork and the both of us fall silent. After a few minutes, I'm completely dressed and am ready to get the hell home. Chopper is waiting next to Ivy. Her shift ended and he's there to pick up his old lady.

"Are you good to ride on the back of my bike or tag along with Bee?" Deeds questions when we arrive at the parking lot.

I lean against him. "The back of your bike."

"Nice. I get to test a little something Vachs added," Deeds says as he places his hand on my lower back and guides me where he's parked his bike.

"And that would be?" I wonder out loud.

Deeds chuckles and leans in to huskily tell me, "I'd rather show than tell you, love."

I groan and hate to admit, "As long as your cock

steers clear of my pussy. Damn, I never thought the day would come I'd voice that sentence."

My mountain of a man grins. "Hard lovin', hard fucking; with you there is no holding back. And I wouldn't have it any other way and yeah, I totally fucking agree. Both pussy and cock need a spa day and I have just the thing to start with."

He straddles his bike and I grab his leather cut to balance myself as I get on behind him. My ass is snuggling closer when he fires up his bike and holy mother of all that's vibrating in blissful desire. The seat underneath me is one huge damn vibrator.

I glance over Deeds' shoulder to see how he pushes some freaking buttons on the handlebar to up the strength of the damn thing. If he thinks this is a way to give my pussy a damn spa day I'm gonna have him drag his freaking bike inside the house so I can ride it every damn minute.

His body plastered in front of me now rumbles with laughter as he peels out of the parking lot. Yeah, there's no damn need to tell the man I'm happy with the…whatever it is Vachs installed…my moans along with his name screaming through the air is all the indication he needs.

CHAPTER TEN

DEEDS

I stalk into church with a file in my hand. It took some firm persuasion, but Lips agreed to crawl into bed and rest for an hour or two while I get things set to take down Ruby and the damn sister.

Lips' last panic attack drained her, plain and simple. Very noticeable 'cause she went out like a light when her head hit the pillow. I also noticed she didn't get much sleep last night. My woman has a heart the size of the world and takes on the weight of the universe on her shoulders along with it.

It makes her perfect, but it also leaves room for stress and other shit to cut in and try to bring her to her knees. Nothing we can't handle, though. We've fought tougher battles and for sure as fuck will overcome this panic shit as well.

First, I'm gonna take care of Rack. The fucker will face my wrath for triggering my woman's latest panic attack. What a damn idiot. Not just for Lips but Lou also doesn't need Rack's idiotic derailment he pulled on her.

I get the fact that he knows shit about having sisters and went straight into overprotective mode, but Lou's a tough cookie from what I've learned about her. You don't tell a woman like that how to handle her business and life.

One glance around the main room of the clubhouse tells me the fucker isn't here. My son is, though. It's also the reason why I came here and I hold the file up to catch his attention and point it in the direction of church. Archer dips his chin and gives his old lady a kiss on her cheek before stalking into church as I follow him in and close the door.

"Everything okay with Ma? Bee basically told me I should focus on my brothers and that she handles the old ladies." Archer winces but I can clearly see the pride on his face.

I can't help but chuckle and gladly tiptoe over the issue 'cause I'm pretty damn sure his mother wants to keep her personal shit to herself. "There's a reason we each have a woman born and raised in Areion Fury MC. They might not hold the same patch as us, but they sure had the perfect president old ladies."

My son grins. "It's why we stole them."

"Fuck, yeah." I grin right back.

We take a seat and I slide the file across the table. "Your mother and I have been working on this case and she's narrowed it down to two suspects. One in particular but since two deaths can be linked to both of them working it's a clear statement both sisters think they can play reaper."

Archer takes the file and quickly scans over the information Lips and I put together the second we got home. I wanted her in bed and resting but we share the same drive when it comes to catching killers so we handled this shit first.

When I was still prez things were different and

I could skip this whole annoying paperwork hiccup until I finished my damn job. That's when I had to sit behind a desk and write a report, but the good old days are behind us for a reason.

Now my son needs to have some paperwork in order to have a safety net in place if things go to shit. Our contact with the government needs to be aware and one simple email, text, or call is enough but it's still a change that wasn't there when I was in charge. Nonetheless, we still get the job done.

"Two? They're both doing this shit? Fucking hell, what a mess," Archer mumbles.

I don't have to reply because he's going over the information and everything is in there. The results of the additional coroner report Lips requested where they checked for insulin and also the link between the two women and the deaths at their work.

Nance, the one working in a retirement home, even volunteers at another retirement home and we've managed to match their time there with all the suspicious deaths so it's a slam-dunk, open and shut case. We only need to take those two in.

Archer closes the file. "We could let local PD handle it."

I raise my eyebrow, even if it also crossed my mind it's not what my woman would want. "You think your mother is going to let you take away the fun part?"

"Fuck," he grumbles. "Fine. But make sure she's not taking them down by herself. And please, for fuck's sake, make sure she doesn't do more damage than usual. Kessie has been giving me shit about how many complications, bills, complaints, fucking mess it is when a case involves Ma."

I can feel my lips twitch. This is nothing new.

"You and I both know it's because she's involved in almost every case and especially when things go to shit," I tell him.

Archer nods. "Like she's born to be in the line of fire."

Again, with the weight of the fucking universe on her shoulders but she wouldn't have it any other way and it's why I tell him, "I'm pretty sure she was born from hellfire itself."

"Truth." Archer chuckles and taps the file on the table. "Okay, take Broke and Depay with you. Should be enough backup to take out those two women. I'll get Kessie up to speed."

Before he gets up I decide to throw another task his way to clear my plate. "One more thing." I wait for my son to nod and let him know, "Your mother has been going to a special place to get her coffee. She's kept the place to herself to create a comfort getaway so to speak. Anyway, long story short, the girl who inherited the place from her mother when she passed away asked your Ma to search for her biological father. Turns out, she's Rack's sister."

Archer's eyes widen. "For real? That's fucking awesome. The man must be ecstatic. Wait. You did tell him, right?"

"We did. Yesterday. This morning Lou, that's his sister, called your Ma to tell her not to come over for a while and make sure Rack stays the fuck away as well."

"What the hell?" Archer mutters and releases a deep sigh. "What did he do?"

I snicker at the fact Archer instantly knows it's Rack who fucked up. "I called to ask myself, but the fucker basically told Lou she needs protection. How she can't open and close her business when she's alone or live by herself in the apartment above the place while running that diner. All while she's been doing it for the last few years, first with her mother and after that by herself."

Archer groans. "I'll handle it. First, I'll have a little chat with Rack and then I'll swing by the diner and make sure Ma can get her comfy getaway back. We all know how much she loves her coffee and I'm sure she was pissed to have this shit with Rack backfire."

Getting to my feet I grab his shoulder and tell him, "Appreciate it."

"Let me know how shit goes with those two angels of death and when I can expect the full report on my desk," my son tells me.

Or make that an order and I can feel the corner of my mouth twitch when I tell him, "Will do, Prez."

I open the door and notice Vachs strolling into

the main room of the clubhouse, Depay and Ganza are right next to him.

"Hey, Vachs," I quip. "Thanks for the tweak on my bike, man. Perfect timing too."

Vachs only grins while Depay and Archer are now bouncing their gaze between us.

It's Depay who questions, "What kinda tweaks?"

Vachs winces and I know exactly why since his old lady is Depay's daughter, Hadley.

I help the brother out by saying, "Vachs here installed some shit so the backseat vibrates. If he needs his old lady to pay attention or whatever, he can hardly call out while riding. Though, I saw other potential and let's just say my old lady was very fucking happy during the ride home."

Ganza chuckles and mutters, "I bet, saves the damn foreplay. I might need you to tweak my bike as well."

We all glare at the idiot. "Who the fuck skips foreplay?" Depay snaps when a confused look slides across Ganza's face.

"I've read about it somewhere. You can control it

with a button and have an option where it syncs with the throttle, right? Sounds like we all need that shit. Make sure you tweak mine first," Archer tells Vachs.

"Mine second," Depay quickly adds.

I shake my head and leave them to handle the "who gets the vibe first" discussion. My bike already has the option to bring my wife some extra pleasure. With a smile on my face, I leave the clubhouse, knowing Archer will handle Rack and this way I get to go home earlier than planned.

Besides, it's Archer's job to handle these things. Hopefully, he can clear everything up and Lips can go back to Lou the way she's been enjoying this option for a while now. I enter the house and it's the silence I'm greeted with that lets me know my woman is still sleeping.

I wander into the bedroom and lean against the doorjamb to enjoy the view. Her long gray hair is spread out over the pillows, almost giving her an angelic look. There's nothing I wouldn't do for this woman. She's been the tight fist squeezing my heart to pump the blood through my veins for decades; the fucker only beats because she's alive.

There's only one woman I love with my whole being. The one who gave me two sons and two daughters and who makes this fucked-up life worth living. We might ride full speed and it's these rare occasions I realize how damn lucky I am to have her in my life.

Realization hits most times when you're being pressed face-down on the facts. I've known from day one how precious and special she is. It's also why we go head-to-head as fiercely because she's my mirrored version, the one who flawlessly matches me in all ways.

"Hey," I croak when I see her blink a few times as she slowly awakes.

"Hey yourself," she murmurs and stretches her arms into the air, making the sheet slide down to expose her magnificent rack.

"I'm gonna head into the kitchen and make you some coffee." Way better than ending up in bed to shove my face between those tits and bury myself deep.

Shit. My cock hardens and the tight confinement of my jeans isn't the most comfortable position to be in when it's still raw from overusing the damn thing. Lips' giggles flow through the air, seeming to know exactly why I'm leaving and it yet again puts a smile on my face.

A few minutes later I have a steaming cup of coffee in my hand as Lips strolls into the room. Tight blue jeans, black biker boots, leather jacket with a black shirt underneath, it's practically her signature look. I hand her the coffee and she takes a few sips, closing her eyes as she enjoys the taste.

She leans against the counter. "Did you clear everything with Archer?"

"I did. Also told him to handle the shit with Rack." She starts to glare at me but I slowly shake my head. "He's the prez and can fuck things up way more for Rack than we can. Besides, I told him how that diner was your special place so even if Rack has to stay away, I'm sure he'll smooth things over between you and Lou."

"Thank you," she murmurs and finishes her coffee.

I nod and continue to debrief her, "Broke and Depay are going with us as backup. I've texted them just now and they should be here in a few minutes so we can discuss how we're gonna handle it."

"Good. We might need two or four more brothers. We need to take them down at the same time. Ruby started her shift when I was at the hospital so she should still be there for the next two or three hours. Her sister is either at home or at work? I haven't checked her schedule yet and we need eyes on her."

"You're right. Let's find out and send a prospect over to check at a distance so we at least have a visual of the other suspect," I agree.

We head for the laptop and at the same time the doorbell rings. I open the door for Broke and Depay and we all take a seat at the table to discuss and make a plan.

CHAPTER ELEVEN

LYNN

"And we're sure Ruby is still at work?" I question.

Dammit. The prospect we sent out to swing by Nance and Ruby's place just called and noticed there's no one home. Nance isn't scheduled to work today either and we have no clue where the woman is. We were hoping to arrest both of them at the same time to prevent either of them from warning the other.

"Positive," Broke quips. "I asked Chopper if his old lady could call a friend who was working if she had eyes on her."

"At least that's something," I grumble, frustrated we can't locate the other one.

"You're lead in this so what's our next move?" my old man asks and warmth spreads my veins.

Stupid because I've been lead in many cases but with the panic attacks–and catching him talking to our son in an effort to make my load lighter–it feels good to know he still has my back. Many of these assholes are overbearing Neanderthals, what happened with Rack is the latest example. Though, Deeds is still right next to me; always and forever.

"I don't want to wait. We know when Ruby's shift ends and I want to take her out without risking others," I tell them.

Broke nods. "We can scoop her up when she leaves the hospital."

"That leaves Nance. We still have no clue where she is." Depay glances over the documents in front of him.

My eye catches the details of the car both women use and an idea strikes. I reach for my phone and tap the screen to put it on speaker as I call Bee.

I can multitask by asking Bee to do something while the others know what I'm up to when I say, "Bee, if I give you the information of a car, can you see if the GPS is active and track it down? I've seen you do it before when they had some kind of insurance that linked their car or something. Can you?"

"Sure thing. I'm already behind my laptop so give me the details," she quips and Depay gives her the details.

It takes a few minutes before Bee says, "It's on the move. I'll send the data to Deeds' phone so he can track it in the app."

"Thanks," we all rumble and I disconnect the call.

"Weapon up, we're getting ready to bring them down. We'll keep an eye on the moving target while we take Ruby down first." I get to my feet and feel the spike of adrenaline that always starts when we're about to take down suspects.

My phone rings in my hand and I see Archer's name flash. Picking up the call I bring it to my ear when I tell the rest of the guys, "Keep in mind these two might kill by using a syringe but who knows what direction they jump in when they are cornered. If you need a reminder…Ruby has a permit for a firearm." Grunts ring through the air and the guys get to their feet to spread out while I tell Archer, "Sorry, had to give those old farts a reminder. They've all been shot and injured too many fucking times."

"Ain't that the truth. Shoot me a text when you have the locations, I might add some backup. 'Cause like you said, you never know what perps do when they're cornered. But that's not why I called. Listen, I handled Rack and made it clear he's fucking up by shoving his newfound sister into a golden cage. I also called Lou and explained the situation. She asked if you could swing by for coffee today or tomorrow and that she already hated her decision and missed you already." Archer chuckles. "She sounds like Esmee and Lynette. I have a feeling she's not just Rack's sister…more like an adopted one of mine."

My chest fills with warmth when his words wash over me. "I had the same feeling when I first met her. Lou's mother was a real sweetheart but it's Lou who reminded me of my own daughters and you know how damn much I miss them. She's not a substitute or anything but–"

"I know, Ma. It's fucking amazing to add good people to your circle and it's damn rare when you find them. Fuck. To know she's even connected to Broken Deeds by blood just shows how much of a rare find she is."

"Thanks for clearing the air. I'll swing by when we have those two killers in custody. Fuck knows I need coffee and something yummy when we finish this job," I tell him.

"Anytime, Ma. Stay safe and if you're okay with it I'd like to go with you to check out Lou's diner later this week."

"Anytime, son," I echo. "Anytime."

We end the call and I suck in a deep breath, slowly letting it out while a smile tugs my lips. Damn, I feel a lot better to hear Archer handled things between Lou and Rack. Time to focus on the mission at hand.

I only have to check my weapons, the one placed

on my hip and my backup gun I have strapped on my lower leg, covered by my boots. We pair up in teams and instead of taking bikes, we take two SUVs and head in the direction of the hospital.

I've texted Archer the details and I haven't heard back yet but I'm sure extra backup will be there without us knowing what or where. The dot of the car stopped moving in the app and it's clear the other sister is picking Ruby up from work.

"Here she comes," Deeds rumbles and we all glance left to see Nance park the car near the entrance of the hospital.

"Broke, Depay, go around so you guys are at their backs when we confront them," I order.

Depay nods. "Element of surprise, got it."

"Something like that," I muse. "Just wait till we address Ruby. I'm sure Nance will get out of the car and when she does you guys are up to cuff her."

"Oh, and Archer mentioned he arranged backup. Haven't heard or seen anything but I'm sure it's some form of damage control." I chuckle and let my gaze slide over the parking lot. "It's not that busy so

I can hardly make a mess unless one of those sisters rips through the parking lot with their car and cause damage."

"Or gets inside the hospital and take hostages," Broke chimes in.

"Let's not jinx shit, you know how creative my woman is," Deeds mutters and leans in to place a kiss on my temple.

I can't help but grin at my man.

"Showtime," Broke snaps and jogs in the direction of where Nance is parked.

Depay follows him and Deeds and I both stalk into the direction of the hospital where Ruby is standing. All four of us are wearing bulletproof vests. Like I told Archer, all of us have been shot or injured in many other ways and we're not taking any chances.

"Ruby Fenlowe," I snap, and her eyes land on me but they quickly slide to Deeds.

The fucking cunt flashes her snatch-dripping smile in my man's direction again and I see red. My hand is on my gun and I'm aiming it at her head with my next damn heartbeat.

"Get a good eyeful 'cause it's the last thing you'll experience in freedom," I snarl.

Shit. Ruby drops her purse but her hand isn't empty; there's a gun aimed right at my chest. Was she fucking expecting me? Us? What the hell?

"End of the line, ma'am. Time to put a stop to it and lower your weapon. There's enough evidence to put you behind bars for life," Deeds tells her from right beside me.

From the corner of my eye, I notice he's also palming his gun, having my back as always.

"Let my sister go," Ruby states as if Deeds didn't just say anything.

I slowly shake my head. "You heard my old man, end of the line. Your sister is going down for the deaths she caused by administrating insulin to patients, same shit you pulled."

A crashing sound catches all our attention. The metal hitting metal isn't hard to guess that there's a car hitting others, but I can't take my eyes off the woman holding us at gunpoint. I hear Deeds bellow, but I also notice a mother and a little kid coming up from Ruby's left.

Ruby sees them too and the thought of her snatching them as hostages slides through my head at the same time Ruby takes a step in their direction. I'm ready to squeeze the trigger but I can't because strong arms surround me and cause me to tumble to the side.

I watch Ruby and Nance's car speed by me, feeling the wind from the speed and how close it's rushing by, before it slams into a parked van. I'm struggling to get to my feet, trying to fire a bullet in Ruby's head before she can do something to the kid she was reaching for but again I'm yanked to the ground.

A bullet grazes my arm and slams into a car behind me while at the same time I see Ruby's head whip back, a red dot appearing between her eyes as she crumbles to the floor. The red dot hovers over her heart for a few breaths before it disappears. Deeds and I both rush forward and manage to block the vision of the dead body from the kid.

Depay and Broke are suddenly in front of us as well, talking to the mother who has her kid wrapped tightly against her chest. They are calming her down as local PD enters the scene with flashing lights.

"Close call," Rack states from behind us. That explains the red dot, he's one hell of a sniper. "Sorry, Lips. I knew this was your case but Archer gave the order to have your back and I made a flash decision to take the remaining target out."

"No need to be sorry," I grit as I grab my upper arm and glance at the flesh wound from the bullet Ruby fired.

If Deeds wouldn't have pulled me out of the way, it could have been way worse. Even if I would have fired a direct hit at Ruby to take her out, in the end, it was teamwork for the win that kept everyone safe. Including the civilians who would have been hostages or worse…collateral damage.

"That fucking bitch jumped back into the car and started firing while hitting the gas," Broke sighs in frustration. "Could have been way worse if we didn't take her out."

I glance around at the destruction. At least eight cars are totaled before Nance crashed into the one that stopped hers.

"You call that way worse?" I snap and point at the mess we're surrounded in. "It's as if you fuckers take a challenge whenever we have a case to solve where I'm the one taking lead. Kessie is going to have a field day with this one. Hell, she might put me on non-active for this shit."

Depay grins. "She wanted to do that last year when you took out that serial killer in front of that Hollywood couple. Good thing Kray yelled 'Aaaand cut, great scene, that's a wrap.' Made those fuckers believe we were taping a damn episode of a biker series."

I can feel my eyes widen. "No fucking way. Archer said–" My lips slam shut when I notice both Broke and Depay studying their boots.

One quick glance at Deeds also shows he's looking anywhere except in my direction.

"What the fuck? The cunt has it in for me, doesn't she?" I snarl.

Nope. No reaction at all, it's like they don't even want to be around me to answer my damn question. It's then I realize Archer has been keeping Kessie off my back for a long time now. Fucking bullshit. When my old man was still president we didn't have to report to the government; they reported to us.

"Whatever," I grumble. "Those pencil peckers know shit about how things go in the line of fire."

The burn on my arm is a vivid reminder along with the flash sliding through my brain of what just happened. Gunpoint, a car missing me as I felt it whoosh by; if it wasn't for Deeds it could have been twice as bad. Not to mention, the panic attacks.

One, or all of it, make me blurt, "I'm gonna retire anyway. I'm getting too damn old for this shit, and I want my ass and face to stay pretty." I glance up at Deeds. "What about you? How about we head back to the island and see Linette and Windsor? We could check out one of those apartments near the beach and buy one to enjoy months of the warmth and sunshine of Ryckerdan and come back here to annoy these fuckers when we get bored of wiping off the sand hiding in our ass cracks."

Deeds grins. "I don't think I'll ever get tired of the crack of your ass."

"Oooookay, that shit is making my ears bleed. I'm out of here," Rack mutters and stomps away.

"Thanks for having our backs, Rack," I tell him with a load of sincerity.

I might have been pissed at him for the way he handled things with Lou, but he was there when we needed him. I'm sure Archer planned it, sending him as our backup without saying anything; giving Rack a chance to redeem himself.

It simply shows how well our son has everything under control. Bee as well with the old ladies. I might have blurted out my thoughts about retiring in the heat of the moment, butt-freaking-hurt but it sounds right. It feels right. Not to mention, my body is screaming at me "it's about damn time." Let those young kids go all out, guns blazing, and handling whatever comes their way.

I lace my fingers with Deeds. "Take me home, stud. I need Ivy to check my arm and after that, we're going to make plans for us to retire in a few months."

"A few months, huh? Postponing? Already regretting the decision?" he questions as he guides me back to one of the SUVs.

"Nope, not at all," I firmly tell him. "But we can't simply pack up and leave this time because I'm fucking serious. We're going to stay in Ryckerdan for months instead of a vacation. That shit needs good planning instead of hopping on a plane."

His eyes widen and he brings us to a stop. "You're serious."

"As a damn panic attack," I grit.

The air rushes from my lungs as he suddenly swoops me into his arms and slams his mouth over mine. I'm digging the full-assault domination, but the man pulls back way too damn fast.

Placing his forehead against mine he whispers, "More time to spend together while changing scenery because we can bug the Broken Deeds chapter we founded there with Spence if we do get bored."

My grin is huge as I shoot him a wink. "Exactly.

At least Kessie isn't their government contact person."

Deeds barks out a laugh as we get into the SUV and head back to the clubhouse. Time for a change is hanging in the air and it smells like a mix of cocktails and beach. Fucking perfect.

CHAPTER TWELVE
A few months later

DEEDS

"Never thought I'd see the day she'd be happy to walk away from her hometown," Zack tells me as we both stare at our old ladies talking to Lou.

A surge of pride hits me. "That's because she's not walking away. She's switching things up. She might say she's retiring but we'll still dabble in Broken Deeds cases. For months she's been taking baby steps back and has turned into a vault of information and advice. When someone hits a dead end, they call and babble. She triggers new leads or a clear head. It soothes her needs while the pressure and stress is off the damn table."

"Perfect solution," Zack murmurs and I turn to face him.

"How is shit going with you guys? You haven't shared anything about retiring yourself and leaving the twins to run the MC."

Zack winces. "Yeah, you might say it's not as smooth as the way it was when you guys retired but it's out of my hands. It's like watching stallions hit a fresh meadow to run free."

A bark of laughter hits me. "You must have forgotten the early years, everyone goes through that phase. Hot and new pussy at every turn, life without worry, and thinking you can handle and damn well know everything."

"Repressed is more like it." Zack chuckles. "Besides, Blue had held my heart since we were kids."

I let my gaze slide to Zack's sister, my woman. Blue and her have been best friends since growing up and living right next to one another. I can't imagine having a taste and then losing her the way Zack and Blue were ripped apart. They have so much history and yet they were given a second chance.

"Funny how life has a way to let paths cross to open up a whole different road for a glance at one hell of a future. Even if the world blew up now it would mean we were graced with some damn fine years," I muse.

Zack leans back in his seat. "We'll make sure the world doesn't blow up 'cause we might be old but our candle isn't burned out yet."

"I've heard enough," Rack grumbles. "You two old farts can reminisce about the good old days and golden years to come but I'm gonna keep living in the now."

"Picking up your old lady, huh?" I quip, knowing his balls are wrapped in a bow the way Zack and I have had them for decades.

The brother shoots me a grin. "Can't keep her waiting. Your old lady might be lethal with her mouth but mine has a sharp eye."

I check my watch. "Then you'd better hurry."

He glances at the clock on the wall and mutters a curse. I'm chuckling when he dashes up and jogs to his sister to give Lou a quick peck on her cheek before he rushes out the door.

"Glad those two found one another, they match in every way," I muse.

"He wouldn't have claimed her if they didn't," Zack adds. "Even if some aren't looking to hand over their heart and balls, it's inevitable when you meet the right woman. Even if it's only one woman for two brothers."

"The fuck?" I grunt.

Zack rubs a hand over his face. "My twins do everything together. Both of them Prez, sharing tasks and I've heard they also share an interest in one woman when they fuck. How the hell is that going to work when they meet the right one? One for both?"

I blink a few times and the first thought that enters my head is, "Kray and North were the same way. They might not be blood brothers like your sons but they found their one and only in identical twins so in the end, it worked out. Who knows what they run into or what life has in store for them? They'll make it work, I'm sure."

"Right," Zack mutters. "Nothing we have to

worry about."

"Right," I echo. "'Cause we're retired and handled enough shit. Time for those young fucks to screw life by the day and see what's cumming."

Zack snorts a laugh. "Cumming."

"What the hell are you two talking about?" my woman quips as she slides into the booth beside me.

"Cum," Zack easily supplies.

Lips wrinkles her nose. "And they say I'm weird."

Blue chuckles as she snuggles closer to her old man.

"Are you all set?" I question and brush my lips against my woman's temple as I pull her close.

"Yes. I'm all ready to go," she cheerfully quips.

This was our last stop before we head out to the airport. Windsor's private jet is waiting to take us to Ryckerdan. Over the past few months, we've made two visits to the island. Once to check out a couple of apartments and the last time to sign and buy the place we instantly fell in love with.

It's going to be our main house while we will

also keep the one we've lived in ever since we got together. This way we can come back here a few weeks a year to spend time with the grandkids.

"Okay, let's hit the road." Zack and Blue slide out of the booth.

Lou wanders over and hands Lips a thermos flask with the diner's logo on it and a paper bag along with it. "Here you go. Something sweet for the road and a special flask to put your coffee in and keep it hot while remembering where you're always welcome to get a better-tasting cup of coffee."

Lips is grinning from ear to ear. "As if I can ever forget. Besides, you already gave me the address where I can order those magical coffee beans."

Lou catches Lips by surprise when she flashes her arms around her to give her a big hug. "I miss you already."

"I'm one phone call away and will be back for a visit soon," Lips promises and adds on a whisper, "Besides, that biker sitting in the corner might fool anyone, but you and I both know he has the hots for you. So, you'll have your hands and brain occupied with other things."

I let my gaze slide to the corner and lift my chin at the fucker; both in warning and in recognition. He might be fooling everyone else by making it seem he's working behind his laptop but the fucker gives me a slight nod, letting me know he has his eyes locked in our direction.

If I read through my woman's words, I'd say Lou will become an old lady soon enough. Good. Another thing my woman doesn't have to worry about. Lou will be looked after anyway with her being Rack's sister but I'm sure Lips will be over the moon if that fucker steps up and claims her.

She's been a matchmaker for many brothers through the years. Her latest victories being Wyatt and Rack. Well, maybe Lou is the one she marked as a going away bonus thing but whatever…we're leaving everything on a positive note.

The ride to the private airstrip is short while saying goodbye to both Zack and Blue does take a while. The sound of bikes rumbling the air draws our attention to the right. Fucking hell. The whole club, first generation and their old ladies, are on the back of their bikes, as the second generation is rolling down the runway. A long row of bikes are parked side by side and a lump forms in my throat.

I glance at Lips to see her eyes are brimming with tears. Yeah, neither of us expected this. They know us too damn well to come and say goodbye again. Especially when we already made sure to visit each and every single one this morning.

We both wave, getting a flow in return as we take the stairs to enter the plane. They all rev their bikes, the sound pulling at our hearts as the door closes behind us. We all know this isn't forever but it still feels like closing a chapter, which basically it is but we're opening a damn new one as well.

A new chapter in our lives and I can't wait to see what's in store for us. Hopefully loads of time will be spent with each other, letting the next generation take on the stress and confrontation life gives while we're always there to support them and give advice.

For we always learn from mistakes, wrong and right decisions, and every pile of shit life throws our way. Good or bad it makes you feel alive to live, laugh, and love hard enough to face another day.

And what a gorgeous fucking day it will be when I now realize we can sleep in without a damn alarm clock waking us to take the next job. Yeah, the only worries we have is...like my woman mentioned... getting the sand out of the cracks of our butts.

Whatever, I'll make sure not to get it there in the first place so problem fucking solved. I grin to myself as the plane slides into the air and I stare down at the row of bikes, brothers, and old ladies, waving us off.

EPILOGUE
Three years later

LYNN

Grinning, I place my phone back on the table beside me and close my eyes as I soak up the early morning sun. I'm lounging on a lounger on my balcony. It's my favorite spot to either read in the evening or relax in the morning.

Sipping coffee while being allowed to close my eyes and drift off for another ten minutes before I start my day. Except, right now I'm not allowing myself to drift off so I'm squinting to keep an eye on the beach.

Deeds was up an hour before I was and most times, he changes into shorts and goes for a run along the beach. Sometimes with Windsor or one of our grandkids but this time he went by himself. It's the whole reason I dragged my ass out of bed and rushed through answering the texts and emails from all the old ladies, the brothers, my kids, and everyone else who keep me up to date.

Another thing I love about retiring and the family we've built over time. My worst fear about moving here is the whole fading away thing. Out of sight, many messages and calls leading to a few, until there's no one thinking we're worth their time.

I should have known better because there's a strong flow of contact between our kids and the chapters of Broken Deeds. Many of the first generation have either moved here along with us or somewhere else to retire, enjoying more free time to spend with their loved ones.

With all the free time on our hands I came up with a task all of us can chip in and benefit from. I love reading the news, either the paper or the internet and so do many of the others. There are articles that catch our attention and if so we throw it into a chat group Kray, North, Depay, Broke, Chopper, Lochlan, Deeds, and the old ladies and all are a part of.

This way we can do some legwork and if it does result in a case of a missing person, or deaths that we can link to a serial killer for instance, we shove the case in the lap of the nearest Broken Deeds MC chapter.

It was the one time Kessie was actually smiling when she heard something involving my name when Archer told her about my idea. The chick even threw compliments my way and right after demanded a full report and immediate implementation.

Didn't matter I told everyone I was inspired by Reva, North's old lady. Before those two got together it was she who flagged cold cases where dirty cops were slacking on the job so she emailed those cases anonymously to Broken Deeds. But they, Reva included, still thought my tweaks to this idea were a perfect plan to put in motion.

We've managed to take down two serial killers, solved five missing person cases, rescued two kids, and exposed two husbands for killing their wives. Not a bad result for the first year. Like I said, we enjoy our free time while still being useful in many ways.

My panic attacks are under control. At least now I can feel the first flares hitting my body and I can manage to get them under control so they don't slide into a full-blown panic attack. It's all about balance and we've managed to find ours by retiring in our own way.

I jolt upright when I notice Deeds jogging down the coastline. A slow smile slides across my face. Damn, I love that man. Not just the physical attraction but it's the whole package. Brain, body, soul, sexiness.

He's my will to move forward each day to explore more time together because he's there for me day in, day out. He's fought even me to get to where we are, saved my life on more than one occasion, and sates not only my needs but also every aspect of my soul.

Doesn't mean he's perfect. His shit still smells,

he forgets to put the seat of the toilet down, complains he can't find the damn ketchup in the refrigerator while it's right in front of him as I hand it to him but he's my kind of perfect.

It's a good thing the man doesn't see me gawking at him. No need to feed the ego when it's already taking up enough space, right? I'm on the balcony and I'm surrounded by glass but it's tinted in a way where I can see through it but from the outside it doesn't show shit.

Deeds had it installed so I can tan my ass and tits without anyone seeing me. Perfection since it also allows me to gawk at my man who still likes to work out every now and then. That reminds me of the time when he still did some MMA training.

Mask on, punching his hands into the air while holding dumbbells…sweat glistening all those inked muscles…yum. Yeah, I'm still lusting after the man who can piss me off just as fiercely as making me love him endlessly.

He's laid his heart out to be worshipped by me and I've wholeheartedly placed mine right beside his. Insane how one phone call where he called me a cunt led to us being here in the golden years of our lives while our kids have grown into our legacy.

I frown when I can't spot Deeds in my vision. Did the man disappear on me while I was daydreaming over the fucker? Sitting up straighter, I glance around to see where he went.

My heart practically leaps out of my damn chest to dive over the balcony when I hear Deeds rumble from behind me, "What are you looking at?"

"Motherfucker," I grumble and let myself drop down onto the lounger. "Can't a woman get an eyeful of her husband anymore? So much that it fucking blinds me so he has the nerve to sneak up on me?"

Shit. Even his laughter is sexy and it makes me glare at him. He slowly inches closer, giving me no other choice but to try and sink deeper into the lounger as he hovers over me. Damn. The man makes my nipples stand to attention and my pussy tingle in anticipation.

I let my tongue trail over my snake bite piercings, loving them ever since I put them back. Deeds watches the movement and I know for a fact the man enjoys every single one of my piercings. He steals my next breath away by slamming his mouth over mine.

His tongue pierces between my lips, demanding entrance as he plunders my mouth. Hot. Demanding. Fire-igniting desire is what this man is capable of as lust starts to dwell inside my veins. I let my nails rake over his back and love the low growl that flows from his mouth into mine.

He's just as hungry for me as I am for him. Both seeking pleasure and not just from the need to get off but from the way we consume one another; always have, always will. Our bodies might not be capable of the shit we used to do but our passion runs hotter than ever.

I start to tug at his shorts, wanting him naked so he can fill me up but it comes to a stop when he catches both my wrists and places them above my head to hold them with one hand. The robe I was wearing has fallen open, exposing me to him completely.

His eyes rove over my breasts, and the appreciation and hunger practically drip from his gaze. I can't help myself when I make those babies shake with a slight wiggle of my spine. There's a slow grin sliding across his face and he slowly shakes his head but doesn't stray from his task.

Nope. The man simply leans down and takes one of my nipples into his mouth. I moan. Loud. Teeth grazing, tongue swirling. Fucking hell it's as if the man is licking my pussy and sucking my clit but instead, he's just teasing one of my nipples.

That's how damn skilled he is…or make that perfectly tuned to make my body sing for this man alone. With his free hand, he lifts my leg to place it over his muscled thigh, opening me up to make a home for his cock. He switches nipples right before I feel the heat of his length tease my opening.

Eyes connect with mine. He lets my nipple fall from his mouth, filling me up in one stroke as he rumbles, "I'm the fucking king of this pussy castle."

Dead.

I'm stuck between a gasp, a moan, and a laugh,

and it makes me most certainly land in heaven. The feelings this man manages to bring out inside me, simultaneously I might add, are making me love him even more. Impossible because my heart is already overflowing.

I clench around him and mutter, "The most important piece...each player in life has one but I'm glad your ego is the size of your cock so you won't ever hear me complain."

His husky rumble of laughter is accompanied by his dick sliding out of my pussy and filling it back up, causing the both of us to moan. Yeah, no freaking complaints here when something feels this good. Past, present, and future, this man will always be rooted deep. Inside my pussy, ass, mouth, and most definitely my heart, where he belongs.

I try to free my wrists but it's useless to fight his strong grip. Raising my hips, I slam myself on his cock just as hard as he's fucking me. A low rumble vibrates from his chest and the second I realize my wrists are free is when he pulls out and easily flips me around.

I'm on my hands and knees on the lounger and I'm gasping for my next breath when I feel his palm hitting my ass cheek. Holy fucking shit. The squeal ripping through the air should alert the neighbors but who cares? Nothing can ruin the pleasure coursing through me when he fills me back up from behind.

His lips are right beside my ear when he says on a hot breath, "I'll never get tired of this pussy. Feels fan-fucking-tastic wrapped around my cock as I pound into you like I need the action to breathe. That's what you do to me, fill me with strength and pleasure to live for my next breath. All you."

He grunts and the sound of flesh fills the air as I feel my orgasm balancing on the edge.

"Give it to me, love. Squeeze the cum from my body while you find your own pleasure. Let me feel you, let me fucking love you the way you love me. Fuck. Yes. That's it…fuuuuuuck," he bellows as pleasure washes over the both of us.

Happiness will never die the way days fade into our past. Bad times hitting the good are like waves in the ocean but every once in a while, you have to take a breath and enjoy the view and the beauty in all of it.

Through havoc is a burning love that will conquer all. I know because I've found mine the way our children found theirs. Hopefully one day even our grandchildren will find theirs as well. An everlasting love that warms your heart for a lifetime, even on the darkest of days.

And I'll make sure we'll enjoy it till the day we die.

THANK YOU

Thank you for reading Lynn's story. Gaining exposure as an independent author relies mostly on word-of-mouth, so if you have the time and inclination, please consider leaving a short review wherever you can. Even a short message on social media would be greatly appreciated.

If you would like to read all the stories
in the Broken Deeds MC world
(first and second generation)
Here's the link to all the books:
books2read.com/rl/BrokenDeedsMC

SPECIAL THANKS

My beta team;
Neringa, Lynne, Wendy,
my pimp team,
and to you, as my reader…

Thanks so much!
You guys rock!

Contact:
I love hearing from my readers.

Email:
authorestherschmidt@gmail.com

Or contact my PA **Christi Durbin** for any questions you might have.
facebook.com/CMDurbin

Signup for Esther's newsletter:
esthereschmidt.nl/newsletter

ESTHER E. SCHMIDT

Visit Esther E. Schmidt online:

Website:
www.esthereschmidt.nl

Facebook - AuthorEstherESchmidt
Twitter - @esthereschmidt
Instagram - @esthereschmidt
Pinterest - @esthereschmidt

Signup for Esther's newsletter:
esthereschmidt.nl/newsletter

Join Esther's fan group on Facebook:
www.facebook.com/groups/estherselite

MORE BOOKS

AREION FURY MC

OHIO MC

BROKEN DEEDS MC

WICKED THROTTLE MC

DEATH BY REAPER MC

LOST VALKYRIES MC

COWBOY
BIKERS MC

THE DUDNIK CIRCLE

PEACOCK
THE FAULTS OF OUR SINS

MARLON
NEON MARKSMAN MC

THE FALLON BROTHERS

UNRULY DEFENDERS MC

FREDERICK

UNRULY PROTECTOR

Swamp heads
SERIES

Printed in Great Britain
by Amazon